THOR

THOR

THE BOHICA CHRONICLES™ BOOK FOUR

JONATHAN BRAZEE
MICHAEL ANDERLE

LMBPN Publishing
PMB 196, 2540 South Maryland Pkwy
Las Vegas, NV 89109

First US edition, October 2019
eBook ISBN: 978-1-64202-510-1
Print ISBN: 978-1-64202-511-8

THOR TEAM

Thanks to the JIT Readers

Dave Hicks
Jeff Eaton
John Ashmore
Peter Manis
Micky Cocker
James Caplan
Diane L. Smith
Kelly O'Donnell
Dorothy Lloyd
Deb Mader

If we've missed anyone, please let me know!

Editor
Skyhunter Editing Team

CHAPTER ONE

Thor

Thor sat at the end of the road, waiting for Charles to return.

The new two-leg wasn't bad, but he wasn't Charles. His friend had told him to stay, which was one of the first human words he'd understood. Once before, back at home, the man had told him to stay and left him for many, many days. But in the end, he'd come back and taken him to this place.

Given time, Thor knew that he would come back again. He didn't know why they couldn't be together forever, but he'd been confused for much of his life, living both inside and outside the Zoo. It had been Charles who had given him an anchor.

He drew in a deep breath to test the air. This place smelled different from home. It was…bland. There was life out there, but not the ever-changing life he was used to.

That dredged up memories of his pack. He felt an emptiness inside him. His very being cried out to be with them. He knew he belonged with the pack. But when Charles had been threatened, he'd immediately reacted. He'd taken on the alpha himself to save his friend. It had almost cost him his life, but he wouldn't hesitate to do it again in exactly the same way.

A stick pelted him on the head, but Thor didn't react. The small creatures had only now gotten up enough courage to approach him, and that only from the heights of the trees. One of them was braver than the others and crept into the nearest tree to throw a stick down before it scampered back, howling in fear, to the protection of the others in its troop.

Thor was not able to laugh in the human manner, per se, but he did appreciate a degree of humor of sorts. The little animal thought it was safe when it approached him, but it evidently underestimated his ability to jump. With one leap, he could pluck it out of the tree and bring it down for a snack. It only had one set of hands and one set of teeth—hardly enough to defend itself from him.

Something stayed his hand. The creature was like a miniature two-leg, a "human," as Charles called his kind. Some of Thor's earliest memories were of the man teaching him, and one of the earliest lessons was that humans were not to be harmed. Thor hadn't followed that lesson, having killed and eaten the man who'd hurt him and two more after that. He loved Charles, but he'd come to think of his friend's rules as suggestions rather than anything hard-and-fast.

The little two-leg in the trees might not be human, but it was close enough that he would let it be.

Thor shifted his weight and continued to stare off into

the jungle. The new two-leg, Achille, had gone off as he did each morning since Charles had left and told him to stay. With no reason to do otherwise, he did. But he was getting bored of this existence. Out there, smells intrigued him. He wanted to explore this new world.

A new smell tickled his senses immediately before a crack sounded. Something hard slammed into his shoulder and bowled him over. He struggled to regain his feet. Something else struck his back and pain lanced down to the soles of his feet. Acting on instinct, he lurched off the trail and under some low, leafy plants where he laid and tried to make sense of the fire in his shoulder and back.

The little stick-throwers fled through the treetops and the jungle went quiet. Thor slowed his breathing and listened. After several minutes, he heard the slow, careful tread of another animal—no, two others. Two humans. They'd been downwind of him and only a stray eddy had brought him their scent. They smelled differently than Charles and more like Achille. But there was something else—something cold and bitter.

Thor had seen the humans kill others in the Zoo, even his own pack. They used metal sticks that smelled the same. He knew these men had used their sticks to strike at him.

"*Nibo ni o wa?*" one of them whispered to the other. Thor was building up a good vocabulary of human words, but these were different. He knew by now that humans used sounds like these to communicate with each other, but none of these were familiar to him.

Instinct prickled and he began to edge deeper into the brush. He had to get away from them, even though he knew he could crush either without a problem. Quite early on, while playing with Charles, he'd realized that he was stronger than any human. But their metal sticks, which Charles called "rifles," made up for their weak limbs and tiny teeth.

The two stepped out of the jungle and onto the trail. Both were as dark as Achille, one young and one old, and both carried metal sticks. The older one knelt where Thor had been hit, touched the ground tentatively, and brought his hand up to his nose. He grimaced, then asked *"Kini eyi? Ejẹ bulu?"*

The younger one looked afraid and began to scan the jungle.

"Ejẹ bulu?

The older one stood and pointed at the ground Thor had just traversed. He adjusted his finger as he followed the trace until he pointed directly at him where he hid in the foliage. The old man raised his rifle and stepped forward cautiously.

There was nowhere for Thor to retreat. If he broke and ran, the human would shoot him again. He was hidden for the moment, but he knew exactly where he was.

The younger two-leg followed, his body tensed for action, but was that to fight or flee?

Thor didn't want to attack the two humans. Charles' message had been driven deep into him. He'd killed before and he would again if he had to, but that didn't mean he wanted to attack them.

On the spur of the moment, he uttered a low growl. The younger human straightened and looked behind him as if he intended to run, but his companion barked something that seemed to steel the nerve of the younger two-leg.

The older human stared into the bushes. He raised his rifle and fired three times. Thor flinched when one of the rounds buried itself in the dirt only centimeters from his left paw. He quit growling when he realized that would only serve to pinpoint his position.

His attacker took a step forward and used the muzzle to push aside the nearest leaves to reveal Thor. His eyes grew wide and he shifted his aim, but the animal did not give him a chance. With a lunge, he jumped forward and his jaws snapped as he struck the old human in the chest and knocked him back. The man fired, but both rounds went over his back.

Thor's jaws closed on nothing, so as he straddled the attacker, he dove for the throat. The human raised his arm barely in time, and his jaws closed on it. He had grown huge and his jaws were immensely powerful. With barely an effort, he snapped the arm like a twig. The human's screams rose feverishly to be swallowed by the green jungle.

The younger began to keen and backed away as he struggled to bring his rifle up. Thor jumped off his first victim and closed the gap within two strides. The man spun to run, but one bite at his thigh hamstrung him. He fell and clutched the back of his thigh as he pushed himself forward with his good leg.

Thor stepped forward and straddled the human, his own wounds forgotten. The two-leg made no effort at all to defend himself. He leaned forward, clamped his jaws around his neck, and squeezed. The man gasped before

Thor twisted his head from side to side, powered by massive neck muscles, and almost severed the head completely. Blood fountained from the wound and flooded his mouth.

Memories of his first human victim flooded his mind. Coppery, delicious human blood, unlike the quasi-gazelles that had been the packs' main source of food in the Zoo. If it weren't for Charles telling him not to kill humans…

"*Abiku*," the older human whispered behind him.

Thor had almost forgotten the two-leg. He spun, but the human sat quietly and cradled his destroyed right arm with his left. His metal stick was on the ground beside him, apparently forgotten.

"*Abiku*," he repeated, his eyes wide with fear.

Thor dropped the younger human, whose head struck the ground with a dull thunk. Slowly, he approached the older two-leg, who merely stared at the apparition that advanced to take his life. At the last moment, before Thor closed his jaws around the man's face, he brought his left hand up to ward him off. It made no difference at all. Hand and head together could not withstand the pressure those jaws could create.

The human squeaked once before his skull crushed to erupt brains and blood down Thor's throat.

He released the body. When he'd killed the other man, hunger had driven him to eat the body. Thor wasn't hungry now because Achille fed him each morning. But the taste of blood and brain excited him. He stood over the body and howled his victory.

Standing over the prone corpse, Thor scanned the jungle. The tiniest of movements caught his eye. Up high in one of the trees, his stick-thrower huddled and hugged the very top branch as it shivered in fear and stared at him. It hadn't fled with the others, but maybe it wished it had now.

This jungle was so different from the "Zoo," as Charles called home. No vines reached out to consume the body and no animals approached to start the corpse on its journey to its next phase. That somehow seemed wrong and wasteful to Thor. Maybe there were other scavengers here in this jungle, or maybe not.

He wasn't hungry, but he couldn't simply leave the bodies there, could he?

With that justification, Thor began to feed.

CHAPTER TWO

Achille

Achille Amadou made his way back to the ranger lodge. It had been a good day. He'd discovered a line of poacher snares and dismantled each of them, and the wires now hung from his belt. There had been a civet in one, long dead, its body mangled by scavengers. He'd felt a tug of regret as he freed the wire from where it had fused with tissue and bone, but at least he'd cleared the death traps from his park.

Yes, *his* park. W National Park, along with Arly National Park and Pendjari National Park made up the WAP complex that straddled Benin, Burkina Faso, and Niger, but to Achille, W was his. From the river to the deepest bush, it was his responsibility to keep it safe. These poachers were bent on destroying this treasure, all for a quick buck. They had no care for the future or for a destroyed environment where their children and children's children could not scrape enough out of the earth to survive.

Achille fought the poachers, the miners, and the farmers, all who would despoil W. Farmers weren't the big problem. Yes, some entered the park to plant their crops and hoped there would be something left to harvest when they returned. He would tear the crops up when he ran across them, but he held little ill will to the farmers. They simply struggled to survive and to feed their families as best they could.

He held the miners in greater contempt, but the problem was not as great in the WAP Complex as it was in places like Sierra Leone, Liberia, Angola, and the Congo, where water was poisoned and miners kept in what was essentially slavery. Even in Benin, the government was able to keep the Chinese cement companies out of the parks, so all Achille had to contend with was the occasional prospector who panned the rivers for traces of gold.

The bane of his existence was the poachers. Individual hunters who sought bush meat to feed their families or sell in the market were often not well-armed and relied on snares like those now hanging from Achille's belt like trophies. They took large numbers of animals, but they didn't actively seek confrontation with the rangers.

It was the others, those who often had military backgrounds and worked for the big-money corporations or the warlords who posed the biggest threat—and earned Achille's strongest condemnation. They captured baby animals for the international black-market and killed the parents to get at the young. Mass slaughter of bush meat animals was common, all intended for sale in the big cities as far away as Lagos. Not only that, they killed to feed themselves while hiding in the jungle.

After the BOHICA Warriors had come in and dealt with the kidnappers of those young girls, Achille had found the carcasses of two elephants, shot and with most of the meat left to rot. The kidnappers had killed both and cut out only the prime pieces.

At least they paid the price, he thought as he patted his FN-FAL, a gift from Mick Bennelong.

He and Mick were kindred spirits, brothers despite being born to different mothers thousands of miles and decades apart.

The BOHICA Warriors. Achille had never met such a diverse group of people, yet with solid hearts. He'd immediately trusted them, which was why he'd agreed when Charles Tillman had returned to the park with…with whatever Thor was.

The bribe might have had something to do with that, too. Booker, the head of the Warriors, told him that their company, acting under the name BCA Conservation Research, Ltd, had been granted an exclusive management contract for a good chunk of the northern part of the W. Achille had initially recoiled, but they assured him it was to protect the park, and they wanted him as their only liaison. He was to tell them what he needed. The thing was, ever since they brought Thor, he had been reluctant to ask for assistance after they paid for the digital radio system so all the rangers could better communicate with park headquarters in the Pendjari. He'd grown fond of the dog, and that was enough for him.

Achille might be a ranger, cut off from most civilization, but he was a man of nature. Without a doubt, he knew Thor was not natural. He had heard rumors of strange doings going on after that alien missile of some years back, and if he had to guess, he'd say Thor was part of that. But Charles had been good to him and he didn't know how to say no. He didn't know if he wanted to say no.

Thor was dog-like—maybe wolf-like—but there were differences. He was smarter, for one thing. Achilles had jokingly started to speak to him in English rather than Yoruba or French, but he was surprised and increasingly sure that the creature understood him sometimes. He certainly understood "stay" and would walk to where the trail led into his station and sit there each day, waiting for something—or someone, more likely—to return.

Each morning since Charles left, Achille fed Thor, who seemed uninterested in hunting for himself, then went out on his patrols. Each afternoon, the animal would be there, and when Achille arrived, he would follow him back to the station.

Achille reached the five-hundred-year-old ìrókò tree that guarded the road junction. Many of the villagers in the region considered ìrókò to have supernatural properties. He was not so sure. It was a tree, after all, but he also felt it was better safe than sorry. He nodded his head at the grandfather tree and gave thanks for it guarding the path to his station, then turned down the path…and stopped dead in his tracks.

An AK-47 lay on the ground, covered in blood. Another was fifteen feet away. The dirt path was soaked in dark-red blood and flies buzzed everywhere. Pieces of clothing were torn and scattered. Fragments of bone and tissue were everywhere, but no large bones.

Lions. Maybe hyenas, he thought as he surveyed the scene.

He should feel shocked. The AKs and some of the remnants of clothing and equipment told him that these were two poachers who had been hunted, rather than being the hunters. It was rare for poachers to be anywhere near his station, but they could have simply been coming up the drive from the highway and stopped for a rest.

Working methodically, he gathered the weapons and whatever else he could scavenge. He'd give them to his director when he made his monthly visit. Hopefully, they would be displayed as a warning to others who tried to poach the park. Mankind might be the apex predators on Earth but sometimes, Mother Nature fought back.

Achille started looking for sign. He wanted to know what had killed the poachers. It wasn't so much that he regretted that they were killed, but if there were man-eaters on the loose, there were innocent people who could fall victim to them. He didn't see much until he located a huge pawprint in the middle of a patch of path where blood had soaked into the dirt.

It was huge, but it wasn't lion. In fact, it wasn't any of the park's normal residents. With a sinking heart, he knew what it had to be. He stepped up, and a hint of something dark caught his eye. Curious, he tilted his head to get a better look. It was dark, almost black, but there was a hint of blue. Charles had mentioned that Thor had blue blood.

Thor did this!

He unslung his FN and peered into the bushes. Charles has assured him that the big beast would not harm a human, but there had been something off, something hidden in the big man's words. Maybe Thor had done this before.

His heart began to race. Achille knew lions. He knew hyenas and he knew hunting dogs and leopards. More than anyone else, he knew the animals in the WAP. He didn't know mutant or alien dogs, though, and he felt very, very vulnerable.

Thoughts tumbled through his brain until he felt he knew what happened. Thor had a habit of sitting within the entrance of the path to his station. Most people passing would not notice him, and even if they did, they would assume he was a big hyena. Poachers take almost anything, however, and a hyena would be targeted if it was seen. Given the splashes of blue blood, they'd shot Thor but he'd turned the tables on them.

Achille couldn't really blame Charles' pet, but he wasn't about to sacrifice himself for a non-native animal. He'd kill it before it could get him or any other park visitor. Or, God help him, any of the villagers out beyond the park boundaries. Achille's job might be to protect the animals of the park, but he was also there to protect the villagers from his animal charges.

Achille walked backward, each step carefully placed as silently as he could. The muzzle of his FN swept from side to side, ready to cut the beast down when it came to him. He was tempted to call out, but he'd just as soon make it back to the station before dealing with it. Thor had killed at least two well-armed poachers, and that was no mean feat.

Step-by-step, he backed all the way to the station. He heard movement to his left and identified it as something pacing him. Whatever it was, it was big. For maybe the first time in his life, Achille hoped it was a lion on his trail.

Every snap of a branch set his hair on end. He wanted to spray the bushes but all that would do would be to empty his mag.

Achille was sixty-five years old, fit and used to life in the bush. He was not a man prone to fear, but right there, right then, he was afraid. Despite that, he had to will his legs to work. He knew if he turned and ran, Thor would pursue him, so he forced his body to face what he was sure was the beast.

His nerve could only last so long, however. When he reached the cleared area in front of the station, he turned and bolted toward the shelter of the building. Something crashed through the bushes behind him and gave him an extra burst of speed. He cleared the three steps in one bound and pushed the door open, sure he could feel Thor's breath bearing down on him.

He almost cried in relief as he rushed into the room and turned to close the door when something big and enormously strong crashed into it, forced it open, and hurled him onto his back. His rifle spun from his hands to clatter against the far wall.

The big beast bounded past him and turned, and his red eyes glared like Satan himself as he stalked up to the ranger. Achille crossed himself, certain this was the end. He'd always imagined he'd be killed by poachers, but to die at the hands of an animal, even one such as Thor...well, that belied belief.

He closed his eyes as Thor leapt forward and held his

breath as he waited. After what seemed like forever, something big nudged him.

Achille opened one eye, afraid of what he would see. Thor, the huge beast, was on his back beside him, his tongue out and legs spread as he waited for the man to pet his belly.

CHAPTER THREE

Thor

Thor was as content as he'd been since Charles had left. The wounds in his shoulder and back were already healing, even if his shoulder itched. His belly was full, and he was back with Achille.

The human wasn't Charles, but he was still okay. He hadn't been completely sure where he stood with the man after he'd killed and eaten the other two humans.

He had been sleeping his meal off when Achille arrived at the scene. Thor sat up, yawned, and started to leave his nice position under a huge tree when Achille tensed, became alert, and held his metal stick out. That confused him, and he stopped before he could reveal himself.

Part of him wanted to somehow communicate with Achille, to tell him that the bad men were gone. Humans, however, didn't seem to be as capable in determining what he wanted to convey as he was of them.

Something about Achille's posture, something about his smell, that didn't seem right, though. He began to follow the human but remained hidden. When he stepped on a branch, Achille wheeled and aimed his rifle at him. Thor flinched and almost ran off, but something prevented him from doing so.

Step by step, he shadowed the man, confused. Something was wrong, but he couldn't understand what it was.

Finally, Achille must have realized it was safe, because he lowered his metal stick and ran to the station. With a yelp of relief, Thor bounded after him, thankful that whatever had bothered him was over.

Charles used to play with Thor, so he recognized that Achille was playing. They reached the station almost simultaneously, with the man first and him on his ass. They both burst through and into the building.

Thor was usually good for a long play time, but it had been a long day and his shoulder itched. So, like a good member of the pack, he rolled onto his back and presented his belly to an alpha...and unlike his alpha in the Zoo, humans had those wonderful hands absolutely perfect for belly-rubbing.

CHAPTER FOUR

Achille

"Bawo ni o se wa," Achille said as Thor padded out onto the porch before he switched to English with a, "Good morning."

The ranger was not fluent in English and he rarely had to use it, mostly to give directions to backpacking foreigners well off the beaten track. But Thor was raised by an American and he understood several English commands, according to Charles. It would be easier on him to teach Thor Yoruba, but this kept him in practice for when he did need English. Besides, if he messed up, he didn't think Thor would notice.

The big…he wasn't a dog, but Achille simply referred to him as one. What else fit? The big dog pushed his front paws forward and stretched with his butt in the air. He could almost hear the animal's spine crack.

Achille reached over absent-mindedly and scratched at the base of one of Thor's horns.

No dog ever had horns like these, he told himself, then pushed the thought out of his mind.

It was better to think of Thor as a dog rather than as some kind of Satan-spawned monster, one capable of killing—and evidently eating—two humans.

While Thor had snored last night, Achille had contemplated killing him. He was dangerous. What if it had been one of the village children who had wandered into the park?

But it was hard to imagine that the same creature who had rolled on his back for a belly rub was anything other than a large, horned dog. And it wasn't like he'd killed an innocent bystander. While they were healing quickly, Achille had seen the two bullet holes in him. The signs were all there. The poachers had seen him and shot him. He had merely fought back. Thor won and the poachers lost.

Slowly, in bits and pieces, a thought began to coalesce. His fight with poachers was like holding the tide back. They kept coming, and the understaffed rangers didn't have much they could do about it. Not that they didn't try—and they often paid the price for trying with their lives.

This year alone, three rangers had been killed by poachers, two of them friends of Achille's. Being a ranger was a calling. It was a dangerous job, and only those who felt stirred to action accepted the badge. It certainly wasn't the pay.

If he hadn't lost his wife and child to malaria years before, he wouldn't stay. If he had known they would get sick, he would have quit earlier and saved their lives.

The world media always focused on Ebola, Lassa, and

Dengue, of which Benin was fortuitously free, but malaria was still the biggest killer. As a new ranger, Achille had brought his wife and baby son to live with him, leaving his five-year-old daughter with his sister so the girl could attend school. Distant from anywhere, when they'd come down with the disease, treatment was too far away to save them in time.

Of course, Achille had blamed himself. He'd let his pride in his position supersede safety for his family. In the process, he'd lost his daughter, too—now grown and living in Marseille—who had never forgiven him for the loss of her mother and brother. But that had been more than forty years ago and now, the park and its denizens were his family.

And poachers threatened them. He hadn't been able to save his family, but he was bound and determined to save the park.

It occurred to him that he had what looked to be a certified poacher killer. The question was if he could be controlled. Could Thor be trained to protect the park? Could he leave the animal life alone? Could he leave innocent people alone? Could he be trained to hunt and eliminate the poachers?

Come on, Achille. Not eliminate. Kill. Can he be trained to hunt and kill the poachers?

Charles has said that Thor was very trainable. The problem was that Achille didn't know what commands he responded to. They'd be in English but still, that left tens of thousands of possibilities.

First thing first, however. He had to see how well he responded to the other wildlife. It would do no good to have an avenging angel if the angel developed a taste for those he was supposed to protect.

Achille looked at Thor's massive head and asked, "Are you ready to come with me today?"

"Heel!" Achille said as Thor snuffled alongside the edge of the path.

Thor ignored him so he checked his notes again. Yes, that was the English word.

"Heel!"

Once again, there was no response. Evidently, Charles had never taught him that command.

"Come!"

Thor immediately stopped what he was doing, looked up, and ran to him with three ground-consuming bounds. He jumped up and down a few times, rubbed his head against Achille's thigh, almost knocked the slender man over, and ran off again.

"He understands 'come,' but not 'heel,'" he muttered. "I'm going to have to train him that."

He felt the length of line he had wrapped around his waist. If worse came to worst, he'd tie Thor up. For now, he'd keep an eye on the dog and bring him back if he strayed too far.

A stick from above hit Thor on the head. The big dog looked up and immediately went back to snuffing along the dirt.

"Ah, Mr. Ogbé, you are playing with fire, I am thinking," Achille called up into the tree.

The small troop of red-bellied monkeys—what the foreigners called the white-throated guenon—always made him smile. Almost hunted to extinction for their beautiful fur, they were making a comeback, first at the Drabo Forest to the south and now here in the Pendjari and W to where they'd been introduced.

A lone male seemed focused on Thor, who seemed to pay it no mind. The interest wasn't smart. The dog would swallow him as an appetizer, if it came to that, and there were other dangers in the forest that could take advantage of the monkey's singular attention to Thor.

Achille led him deeper into the jungle and the guenon screeched a challenge. The ranger felt alive when he was alone in the bush. Not for him were the stations in the Pendjari and nearer the population centers, where ecotourists hiked and hoped for a glimpse of a rhino, elephant, or lion. The rangers in those stations had to act as crosses between traffic cops and tour guides. Achille ran into the occasional backpacker and school trip, but for the most part, it was him and the animals—and the poachers.

The entire WAP Complex was stunning, but with the river and the mountains of the Atakora Range, he was sure that the W was not only the most beautiful part of Benin, but of all West Africa. If there was a Garden of Eden, then surely it was right there.

All of Benin's old growth had long been cleared, but twenty-two percent of the forests were now protected, a number seared into Achille's mind and a matter of great pride, and the protected areas were making a comeback. Maybe years from now, the Garden of Eden would return. People like Achille had dedicated their life to it.

An *alagbẹdẹ*—honey badger in English, he reminded himself—ambled across the path, and Achille started to call for Thor but decided he wanted to see what would happen. Small but full of fight, a honey badger would not back down to a lion, if it came to that. They were fearless.

The dog's ears perked up when the animal made its appearance. He trotted forward but with curiosity rather than the body language of an animal on the hunt. The badger stopped when it sensed something approach. It darted forward a couple of inches—its danger sign. Thor didn't seem fazed but advanced toward the stubborn creature.

Achille was about to call him off. He didn't think the honey badger could do him much damage, but even a bite could be painful. Suddenly, the creature lost its aggressive stance. It stood up to get a good look at Thor, turned, and scurried away into the underbrush. The dog watched it go before he looked at the ranger as if asking for an explanation.

Honey badgers never scurried off. They faced each danger and put a bad-tempered set of teeth between a predator and itself. They never exposed their more vulnerable back and hind end.

"What did you do to Mr Alagbẹdẹ, Thor? What did you tell him?" Achille asked.

While he knew the animals were notoriously nearsighted, there was no way the creature could have missed him.

The two continued down the path to where it opened into a wide, grass-covered creek bottom. Benin was in the dry season, and the creek was a gathering place for multiple species of animals. A small herd of a dozen kob startled at their appearance and ran off. They were middling size for an antelope but fleet footed. With their head start, Achille didn't think Thor could run one down, so he watched the dog closely. He showed interest but didn't leave the man's side.

The ranger was relieved but he was more interested in how Thor would react to some of the larger animals. Smaller herbivores would probably flee the big dog, but lions, hippos, elephants, and buffalo would almost assuredly hold their ground. Achille couldn't go further with his still half-formed plan until he knew how he would react to them.

He didn't have long to wait. As they walked along the creek bed, they came upon fifteen cape buffalo—twelve adults and three calves—in the mud at the side of the creek.

Thor hopped up on his hind legs, his gaze riveted on the wallowing creatures, and they immediately noticed him. Five of the adults moved to position themselves between the calves and the two interlopers, their tails thrashing the air.

Under normal circumstances, Achille knew this was time for a discreet withdrawal. *Eyẹ Kapu* were mean-tempered brutes, able to drive a pride of lions off. But he wanted to see what would happen. At one thousand kgs, they didn't have much to fear from a dog even as big as Thor. The question was how he would react.

Thor dropped down to all four feet and trotted toward the buffalo. Achille was tempted to let the dog learn a lesson but reconsidered.

"Come, Thor," he shouted out.

He stopped and looked over his shoulder at Achille.

"Come."

The dog took one more look at the buffalo before he turned and trotted back to him. Achille patted his head and pointed at the buffalo, who were still transfixed by the two of them.

"Friend," he said. "Do not hurt."

Thor sat, cocked his head, and looked right into his eyes. Achille could swear the dog actually listened to him.

"Friend."

He caught hold one of his horns and gave it a little tug to adjust their path to give the buffalo a wide berth. The five guard animals shifted to keep themselves between the calves and the two of them, but they didn't show any signs of aggression as they passed the herd.

"Maybe this will work, Thor," Achille said as they continued down the creek bed. "Good boy."

The ranger kept his senses alert as they headed down to the river. It was mid-morning, a little late for hippos to return from grazing during the night, but it was a very stupid idea to get between a hippo and deep water. Many had been killed for making that mistake.

They reached the river without incident, however, and five hippos were in the water, their noses and ears above the surface. Each of them swiveled to watch them, but Thor didn't react. A red pentila butterfly flitted by, and that was much more interesting to the big dog, who followed it. The butterfly landed on a reed, and Achille half-expected him to snap it up, but he was content to merely sniff the insect.

It was hard to imagine that this gentle-seeming creature had killed two humans the day before. Not only killed, but evidently consumed, bones and all. Achille should, by all accounts, be afraid of the dog. But he wasn't. Rather, he felt safe.

The butterfly flew away, and Thor sat and looked at Achille. He wagged his tail and made a heavy thump on the dirt with each stroke.

"You are a strange creature, Thor," he said.

He wagged his tail faster.

A crash made Achille jump and unsling his FN. A huge matriarch stood not twenty-five meters from them as she pushed out of the trees. Behind her, another six or seven elephants tried to see why she'd stopped.

"*Erin, Achille,*" he muttered and reverted to Yoruba as he chastised himself.

In his foolishness, he'd made a rookie mistake. He'd been focused on the hippos and Thor and forgotten that the park was home to more than a thousand elephants—behemoths that needed vast quantities of water each day. He'd let his guard down. With his back to the river, he was trapped.

The matriarch spread her ears and lifted her trunk, signs that she might charge. Achille looked over his shoulder. The hippos wouldn't let him jump in the water and simply swim past, and even if they did, there were undoubtedly crocodiles lurking as well. But if the matriarch charged, he had no other choice.

"Easy, Madame Erin," he said and held one hand out. The elephants in the park were used to humans in safari vehicles, so his smell wouldn't send them into a panic. But that didn't mean he was safe.

Thor took three steps forward, and the matriarch snorted in surprise, then lifted her trunk higher.

"God save us, she hasn't smelled anything like you, Thor," Achille said as he stretched his hand out to grab the dog's tail to pull him back.

It was like trying to move a statue. Thor had his feet planted as he stared at the immense beast. The dog gave a small yip, and the matriarch took a step back. Her ears slowly returned to normal, which was generally a good sign. Achille slowly released the breath he hadn't realized he was holding.

Too soon, apparently. A calf—not even a year old from the look of it—ambled from under the matriarch and charged forward, its tiny ears flapping. Several of the other adults crowded forward, and Achilles tugged harder on Thor's tail. It was time to risk the hippos.

The dog remained like a rock. He was laser-focused on the little warrior who charged, stopped, and charged again while it trumpeted to the world that it was there to protect the herd.

Achille gave one last heave on Thor's tail, but his hands slipped and he fell, landed hard, and knocked his breath out. Dazed, he pushed himself up on his elbows while he fully expected to see the wrathful matriarch thunder forward to squash Thor and him.

She'd taken a step forward as the little one reached Thor. A little bull, Achille noticed, not that it mattered. It was the matriarch who would kill them.

The calf stopped a couple of feet from Thor and his

trunk snaked out. The ranger could hear it snuff the air as it tried to identify exactly what he was.

For his part, the dog stood silently while the trunk inched closer and closer until it touched him. The calf jerked it away, then reached out again slowly. This time, he took a tentative step and snaked his trunk around Thor's neck.

He turned his head and licked it, his blue tongue as big as a python. The little one moved forward and gave him a light head butt.

The big matriarch now moved, and Achille scrambled to get to his feet, ready to bolt. But she ambled forward, her ears flat, and made no attempt to charge. She passed the three so close that Achille could have touched her. As if on signal, the rest of the herd moved through the trees. One of the females grabbed the little bull with her trunk as she passed and hauled him along with her as they made their way to the water's edge.

The hippos moved to deeper water and out of their way, exactly as they should. No one stood up to elephants.

But Thor had, and the two of them were still alive.

Achille was in shock. He'd been a ranger for more than forty-five years and he thought he'd seen everything. Yet he hadn't seen this. He'd never even imagined it.

"Just what are you, Thor?" he asked as his heart tried to slow down.

Thor merely wagged his tail.

CHAPTER FIVE

Thor

He stood at the edge of the bank and watched the big creatures as they rolled in the water. Of course, he had seen larger animals, but not many. These smelled of ancient traditions, going much further back in time than those in the Zoo. The old female reeked of wisdom.

Not so the little one. Full of vim, he had approached him fearlessly, first with outrage, then with curiosity. Thor had been curious, too. He'd let the little one touch him and he'd licked him in return, savoring the established permanence that was so lacking in his own kind. They would walk the Earth many generations from now while he…who knew what his kind would be? They were always changing and constantly evolving.

"Thor, come!" Achilles said.

Thor took one last look at the creatures before he trotted obediently after the two-leg. The man hadn't said so, but he knew the creatures were friend.

Achille made his sounds, most of which had no

meaning to him. Thor knew many of the sounds—stay, come, no, good boy, friend, human, Zoo. Then there were easier ones—Charles, Booker, Roo, Achille, Thor.

He had tried many times to form the same sounds, but his tongue got in the way and his mouth didn't want to cooperate. Still, he was stubborn. Someday, he would succeed. The humans were exceedingly dense and couldn't understand what all other creatures seemed to be able to, so if he wanted to be able to communicate with Charles, he'd have to learn the human way.

The man stopped for a moment and looked back to where they'd come from, and Thor was afraid he wanted to return. He'd been afraid of the big creatures, Thor knew, although he didn't know why. If he returned, he would follow, but he wanted to explore. This place was so different than the Zoo. So stable and maybe even boring, but it was new to him and he wanted to see what was there. The scents that reached him were tantalizing, and he had a compulsion to find out what created them.

He was relieved when Achille turned away and walked along the river. Flying creatures swooped over the water, and others jumped out to flash silver in the sun before they splashed back. So much water awed Thor. Back in the not-Zoo, when he was with Charles, and after that in the Zoo, there had never been so much water. Water in the not-Zoo came in bottles and was poured by Charles into a dish for him to drink. In the Zoo, there was standing water, but shallow and muddy puddles, there one day and gone the next. No one had to tell him that this river had been there for ages and would still be there long after he was gone. He simply knew it.

"*Wara*...uh, hyena," Achille said and pointed to creatures vaguely like Thor but smaller and with sloped hind ends.

Three of them stopped to stare at Thor before he made a high-pitched whine and all three slunk away. They paused every few steps to look over their shoulders to see if he was following. He was tempted, but he knew Achille would get agitated and was content to stay with the human for now.

"*Ijakumo*," Achille said and pointed to a small, doglike creature. "I mean jackal."

Each time they saw a new creature, Achille stopped and made his sounds. Thor tried to remember each one, but he was still unsure as to their meanings. Was the "mongoose" that one small animal that scurried across the path, or were all such animals "mongoose?"

It had taken him a long time to realize that Charles was only Charles and not only human. Booker, Roo, and Achille were all human too, exactly as Thor had been part of the pack but was also Thor, and the alpha was the alpha.

What confused him more was friend. Charles had made it clear that all humans were friend, and Thor thought he understood that. But one human had attacked him in the not-Zoo, and yesterday, two more had. He had killed and eaten them. So, were they both friend and food? He hadn't quite worked that out yet.

"Ah, lion," Achille said and grasped one of Thor's horns quickly to stop him. "*Kiniun*."

Thor had been aware of a strong scent from in front of them for some time, and he was curious as to what created it. But with the grass, he couldn't see. Although much smaller than him, Achille was taller, and he brought his hand up to shade his eyes exactly as Charles used to do.

The dog sat on his haunches, then stood. Ahead of them were seven of the creatures—a huge one with a black mane, three smaller ones without the mane, and what had to be three babies. All lounged in the shade of a large tree.

Thor dropped to his feet, then leaped up on the trunk of a fallen tree. Standing there, he could see them better... and they could see him. One of the maneless adults heard him, and with a chuff, woke the others.

"Stay," Achille said as the adults all stood to stare across the grass at Thor. He held his hand out to grab Thor's tail again, not pulling but ready to.

Thor ignored them. Unlike the steady power of the large creatures by the river, the lion emanated a more nervous power, a more aggressive power. And they didn't like him there.

In the Zoo, there were creatures that disliked all others, despite the undercurrent that connected them all. He knew that the lion was the same. The one with the mane roared and made the three babies scurry for cover. It was a challenge.

Thor understood size as generalities. The maned lion was about the same size as he was. His curiosity made him wonder which one of them was stronger and which one would prevail in a fight. He started to step closer along the top of the fallen tree, but Achille tightened his grip on his tail.

While he could easily break free, he stopped. The lion roared once more, and without thinking, he raised his head and howled. To his surprise, that seemed to startle them.

First one, then another slunk away into the grass. The one with the black mane held steady for a long moment before it, too, turned and disappeared.

"I would not have believed it, Thor. First the Madam Elephant treats you like one of them, then the Mr. Lion backs down."

Thor understood Thor and lion, but the rest was gibberish.

"Let's go home. I think we've had enough for one day."

He understood home. Achille wanted to go back. There was still so much out there—so many scents that he wanted to track—but he would stay with the human.

Regretfully, he took one last draught of air and savored the scents that tickled his senses and massaged them, but a tiny whiff of one triggered concern. It was human but underlying that was the odor of metal sticks and death. One or more humans were out there, humans who had killed.

Friend or food? Thor wondered before he turned to follow Achille home.

CHAPTER SIX

Achille

"Are you ready?" Achille asked Thor.

The animal opened his mouth and uttered a half-growl, half-whine. He laughed and asked, "You trying to talk to me?"

He'd become very comfortable with the dog over the last week. Not once had Thor chased any of the park animals, and most of them seemed to accept his presence, if warily. Only the lions, hyenas, and jackals seemed to go out of their way to avoid him. Achille was curious to see how leopards or the park's few remaining hunting dogs reacted to him.

There was still a big test ahead, though—people. He had to remind himself constantly what happened the last time Thor and other people interacted. His ranger station was one of the most remote in the park but at some point, he'd have to interact with others, and he didn't know what they'd think of the giant horned dog with red eyes—or what Thor would think of them.

There was a chance that time would come soon. He had received a message that there were signs of encroachment into the park.

Unfortunately, there was always encroachment. Poachers, gatherers, or the occasional foreign hunter straying into the park from the adjoining Djona Hunting area—complicit with the local guides who would do anything to ensure their rich clients obtained their trophy. Then there were the odd backpackers who trailed the single highway that led through the park for a hundred kilometers to Burkina Faso. It wasn't particularly safe. Bandits and terrorists had been known to kidnap tourists and hold them for ransom, and there wasn't much the understaffed rangers could do about that.

Achille tried to stay out of the way of the various criminal and revolutionary groups that passed through the park. He was there to protect the animals. If an innocent was at risk, he'd act, but the warlords, drug runners, and other criminal elements were the responsibility of the army and police—which meant those elements acted with what was essentially immunity, passing between Burkina Faso, Niger, and Benin as if the borders didn't exist.

Now, though, he had been ordered to scout one of his areas. The orders came from the ministry in Cotonou which, while not the official capital, was the seat of government. Achille wondered why the attention from on high. His gut told him it might be related to the rescue of the schoolgirls earlier in the year. The BOHICA Warriors had kept his participation low-key and to the best of his knowledge, only the president and his personal aide knew of his involvement. This, he knew, was the only reason he was still alive. If his part in the rescue had become public, he'd have been the subject of a midnight visit—one from which he'd never have lived to see the dawn.

A lone ranger, even with a huge dog, would not be a threat to one of the terrorist groups, and he was assured that he wasn't expected to take any action against them if they had moved into his area. But, as Modeste Loko, his boss, told him, Achille was a master tracker and all he was supposed to do was to confirm if a large group was there or not.

Achille didn't think any of the bigger groups had moved in, or if they had, were still there. Not during the dry season when movement was easy and they could be more readily seen from the air. No, if someone was moving in, it would be poachers, who would target the watering holes and creeks.

He glanced at Thor. The dog was eager to get going. If it was poachers, could he set him on them? Should he? He didn't want to ask himself that yet.

"I hope you can keep up," he said.

Thor was obviously powerful, but they'd travel a fairly long distance to get to the area. He didn't know if the dog would have the endurance. If he flagged, he would have to stop and bring him back.

Achille wheeled his bicycle forward and checked the chain. Satisfied, he swung his leg over the seat and settled his butt in place. He had a thirty-kilometer ride in front of him, and his skinny ass was getting too old for this.

The rangers had vehicles—some old and barely running and some brand-new, donated by NGOs. Achille was out on the long tail of the station network, and the only vehicle he'd ever had was now a rusting hulk behind the station. He usually didn't miss having a car. With only one road and the bush mostly impassible, feet were the preferred mode of transportation—or his battered bicycle.

Maybe I need to ask Booker for a Land Rover.

It would make travel easier but it could also make him the target of thieves.

"Let's go, Thor," he said, pushed off, and headed down the trail.

Mr Ogbé was there, of course, and pelted them both with sticks when they passed beneath him.

Achille needn't have worried about Thor. The big dog didn't even look winded when the ranger pulled off the road and onto a small game trail.

Unlike the human, whose butt ached, legs ached, and back ached. Maybe he did need to consider a transfer to one of the bigger stations down south at Pendjari, one with a nice soft chair where he could answer questions from tourists.

He hid his bike off the path. If he knew the game trail was here, so would others, and a bicycle simply laying there in the bush would be considered fair game—and it would be a long walk back.

"Now, where would they be if they were here?" Achille asked himself before he looked at Thor. "Can you smell anyone?"

He took a couple of big sniffs as if demonstrating and laughed at his foolishness. Maybe that transfer would be a good idea. He was standing there, in the middle of the bush, talking to a dog.

Achille already knew where he was going. If the report were valid and he was not off on some wild goose chase so a paper-pusher could report what he was doing to combat the criminals of the world—when more than a few of those paper-pushers were already in the hire of said criminals—there were four likely locations. It should be fairly easy for him to confirm their presence.

That would, however, have to wait until tomorrow. It would be dark soon, and he was beat. It was time to make a camp and rest for the night.

It didn't take long. After several thousand times, it became routine. Clear off a small section of ground, run a tripline around the camp, set up a fire—whether he actually used it or not—check his FN, and settle in for the night. No South African kraals—only a minimal signature.

He took food out of his pack, shared it with Thor, and laid back. After a few minutes, the dog crept up beside him, and he fell asleep.

The first potential position was a bust. It had taken almost two hours to reach it, but there was no sign that anyone had been anywhere near it in at least a month. Achille's heart almost jumped through his throat when Thor flushed a river hog that bolted, squealing, but otherwise, the area was deserted. With three more places to check, he might be able to reach two more today. That would mean another night sleeping in the bush, check the last place, and a long bicycle ride back. The thought made him groan. Maybe a truck carrying goods from Burkina Faso would drive past and he could catch a ride.

He looked at Thor who nosed happily in the dirt.

No, I guess not. Hard to explain you.

"Come, Thor," he said as he got his bearings and started off.

The next target was probably less than an hour away. Another game trail led to it from the road, which made the trek relatively easy. It also boasted some of the densest forest in this part of the park, which made for good overhead concealment.

Achille headed off into the bush. This was fairly dangerous trekking. With so much vegetation, if would be easy to come up on elephants or cape buffalo by surprise, and that wasn't an appealing idea. But the only alternative would be to continue on the previous game trail for another couple of kilometers, turn onto another, and continue even farther along on a third. That would add at least three more hours, and that didn't thrill him. No, cross-country it was. He'd merely remain watchful and on high alert and hope Thor would sense anything near them.

The African sun climbed higher into the sky and baked the thick brush. There was no breeze, and Achille soon sweated profusely. The lack of a breeze had another disadvantage, however—it wouldn't carry their scent to whatever wildlife might be ahead of them. In times like these, he usually sang and banged the stock of his FN against trees and bushes to give cape buffalo and others warning that he approached. If he was looking for signs of intruders, however, that would be a good way to draw a bullet.

Other than birds and a few monkeys overhead, the two did not run into any of the park's larger animals, much to his relief. He loved the animals, but he wanted to be able to see them from a distance.

They started down the hill to the hollow Achille thought could be a refuge for interlopers when a tiny eddy of flat air whispered around him and died, but not before it brought him the slightest hint of smoke.

He froze and his ears strained for any hint of people. Thor brushed past him, his attention riveted forward. Achille grabbed his tail, which had rapidly become his standard course of action. The big dog didn't seem to mind it, though, and stopped to look over his shoulder at him.

Thor was a huge beast and seemed to have no inclination to move silently through the bush. Either he felt very secure or he hadn't had the need to learn to hunt silently. In this situation, that was a decided disadvantage. Achille had to move forward, and he didn't need the big dog to tramp alongside him and literally crash through the vegetation.

He stepped beside the animal and in a low voice, said, "Stay! Stay!" Thor cocked his head and looked at him, and Achille added another, "Stay," for good measure. He stepped past the dog, and while Thor's body-language screamed his desire to move forward, he sat obediently.

"Good boy, Thor."

The ranger took a few steps forward before he turned to check on Thor, but the big dog hadn't moved. He gave a tiny whine and looked at him with hopeful eyes, but he stayed put.

At least that's taken care of, he told himself as he began to pick his way forward, using forty-five years of experience to move like a wraith, unseen and unheard.

As he grew closer, he began to hear the slightest sounds ahead, almost lost in the hum of the bush. Not many would be able to discern them, or if they did hear them, attribute them to anything out-of-place. But he lived in the bush and he knew her heartbeat. This didn't belong.

But whoever they were, they were skilled. Too many took to the bush, thinking it their birthright, but they were as out of their depth as they would be had they been born in London. Cotonou, Lagos, or Ouagadougou did not teach the ways of nature.

And I'd be as out of place in any of them.

Achille followed a cautious pattern in which he advanced ten or fifteen meters and stopped to listen for a couple of minutes. As he slowly closed the distance, he became more cautious. He knew they were there—at least a dozen or more—and twice, he heard the familiar chambering of a round. This wasn't merely a villager on the hunt for bushmeat for the pot or sale in the market.

He could leave, report back, and let the bigwigs decide if they should send in the army or police. One ranger was not enough to do anything about them, and if they had taken such steps as they clearly had to remain hidden, they'd not take too kindly to him spying on them.

Still, all he had were generalities. If he could only move a little closer and get a visual, he could recognize the regional militaries. He didn't think the Nigerians would come this far over their border, but the Niger and Burkinabe were only a stone's throw away.

Not that he expected national soldiers. The region had

a multitude of ethnic militias and warlord armies. Many wore discerning items such as a colored scarf that branded them. Achille knew most of the armed groups that worked in the area, and if he could only catch a glimpse, that would serve his bosses well.

He had to go slow, however. Even a small mistake could be fatal.

You are a ghost, Achille. A ghost.

The ranger rounded a dense bunch of two-meter-high grass when, from the corner of his eye, he caught the slightest movement up ahead under a sausage tree. Achille turned to focus on it and raised his FN, but the lookout had seen him first and aimed at him.

"Stupid," he hissed as he dove back to the grass, but the sentry fired before he had cover. A searing lance of fire in the back of his leg almost took the breath from him. He landed hard and scrambled into the grass as the man fired twice more.

Achille rolled over and grasped the back of his thigh. He'd been hit, and blood soaked his trousers. Cautiously, he raised his leg and was relieved when it worked—the femur had not been hit, nor his femoral artery. He wouldn't bleed out in the next minute, but that wasn't his main concern. The lookout was shouting for the others.

Of course, if they were skilled in the bush, they'd have sentries in place. He'd been complacent, and that almost cost him his life. It probably still would.

The interlopers were in the riverbed a hundred meters ahead where the cover was the thickest. The lookout had been under the sausage tree twenty meters or so from him. If the man waited for reinforcements, Achille had maybe a minute. If he came on his own, he had only seconds.

He reached for his FN…and it wasn't there. In a panic, he turned onto his hands and knees, gasped at the pain, and patted the crushed grass in search of it. He'd had it when he was shot, so it had to be there.

"You looking for this, Ranger man?" a heavily accented voice speaking Yoruba reached him.

Achille looked up from the path he'd created in the flattened vegetation. A man in military-style fatigues stood at the opening, his foot on the FN. His accent was not Beninese, and his fatigues were not from any of the surrounding nations' military. Achille didn't recognize the rifle aimed at him, only that the muzzle looked extremely large.

He contemplated trying to dive to the side but he knew that would be fruitless. An old man with a hole in his leg had no chance against the young and obviously very fit man holding down on him. His only chance was to try to talk his way out of this mess.

"Yes…yes, I was. I dropped it when you accidently shot me."

The man kicked his head back and laughed a deep throaty laugh and said, "It was no accident, old man. The only accident was that I didn't kill you with one shot. I must be losing my touch."

"I have no disagreement with you, sir. I was merely passing through."

"Ah, but I have a disagreement with you, ranger."

He looked over his shoulder and called to someone or others unseen, "It's a ranger, tracking us. I'll take care of it.

You made a mistake, old man. Now, you will pay." He turned back, raised his rifle to his shoulder, and aimed at him.

"No!" Achille shouted and held a hand up in protest as if it could shield him.

The man gave his head a little half-shake and time seemed to slow for the ranger. He could see the man's finger tighten on the trigger and knew his time had finally come. In only a few moments, he'd see his wife and boy, he realized.

A dark shape hurtled into his field of view and thrust the man aside in the same second that the rifle fired. He fell and landed with a thump out of Achille's sight. His scream was horribly high-pitched and shrill before it was suddenly cut off.

CHAPTER SEVEN

Thor

Achille had said, "Stay." Thor knew what that meant, but he'd sensed humans ahead. He didn't quite know what made one human a friend and another food, but the hairs on his back had stood on end when their scent reached him.

Still, stay was stay. So he sat and a soft whine escaped his throat as Achille disappeared into the bush. He focused his hearing and nose and tried to gather more information on who those two-legs were. Twice, he stood and started to follow but each time, he sat again.

He listened to Achille's footsteps as the human moved farther and farther away. The man was quiet but his ears were keen. Even keener was his sense of smell, and while Achille was alert, he didn't smell of fear. Maybe these humans were friends.

The shots jolted Thor to his feet, and before he realized it, he sprinted forward in a mad dash, stay long forgotten. He didn't consciously track Achille's trail—his subconscious took care of it as he hurtled through the bush, intent on reaching his human whom his instincts told him was in danger.

He heard shouting in the distance, but there were sounds from much closer. Thor rounded a thicket to see a human standing near a clump of tall grass, pointing a metal stick into it. The smell of blood—Achille's blood—reached him, and a sense of fury overtook him. This was a food-human, not a friend-human.

"No!" Achille shouted from out of sight as Thor launched himself at the attacker while a growl rose from the depths of his throat. He pounded the man high in the chest at the same moment that his metal stick fired. The impact took his target out of reach of his snapping jaws, but the food landed hard and bounced. Thor bit down on the human's shoulder and the man screeched in fear. With a jerk, he hitched the human, and the adjustment enabled him to shift his bite to his neck. With one snap, it was over.

Blood filled his mouth, and he instinctively raised his head to howl when shots rang out. He could hear rounds zip past his head like hornets. Humans raced toward him, shouting and firing their rifles.

Thor cut his howl short and began to charge forward when a round clipped one of his horns and snapped his head around. He planted his two front feet, pivoted to the left, and dove into the grass.

He'd let his anger drive him and that had almost gotten him shot again. The innate compulsion raged within, exactly as he'd felt it in the Zoo when all the animals swarmed the humans in a mad desire to rend and destroy them. However, people had taught him something. Those with discipline—like Charles, Booker, and Roo—could hold off any attack when they didn't let their fury take control.

It had been almost impossible to fight off the fury the scent of a plucked Pita plant elicited in all the animals, but this was different. He could fight it. Thor struggled to dampen his emotions, but he felt a wave of cold, calculating anger take over. He intended to kill all these food-humans, but he also wouldn't blindly give them a chance to shoot him.

Thor looked in the direction where he knew Achille was, but he didn't have time to check on his friend. The food were very close, and there were many of them.

He didn't need to see them to know where they were. They were easily pinpointed by their voices as they shouted at one another. He could also smell them.

One was closer than the others. Thor pushed through the grass and despite his size and his usual noisy passage through the bush, he barely disturbed the stalks. He waited, his excitement rising, until the human moved even with him. He darted forward out of the tall grass and bit the man on the thigh. The food yelled in surprise and Thor reversed direction and hauled him back into the cover of the tall grass.

The human tried to bring his rifle around to fire at him, but the animal shook his head to tear muscle and tendons and render the efforts futile. More shouting issued from the rest of the food and some fired their rifles, but Thor only cared about the one he'd caught.

The food lost his rifle in the struggle, and he released the leg to move up and straddle him, his jaws barely inches from his face. Unlike the first one, this food didn't scream. Instead, he reached for a knife in a sheath. Thor instinctively bit down on the arm and broke it cleanly.

"*Bìlísì*" the human whispered before he bit off half of his head.

Thor swallowed, the brain matter a nice counterpoint to the coppery human blood, but a sliver of bone stuck between his teeth. He swiped with a paw in an attempt to free it when more shots were fired. One struck the body in front of him and gouged a hole in the chest.

The humans maneuvered outside the grass and continued to yell at each other. The bone splinter forgotten, Thor took stock of his situation. The area of tall grass wasn't large and the food-humans would be able to surround him. Achille was only two bounds away, but he couldn't go to him. Doing so would draw the men there. Staying where he was wouldn't work either. The food would draw closer like tightening the noose on the quasi-gazelles at the Zoo. He had to break free before it was too late, both to lead the food away from Achille and to create room of his own to maneuver.

He was not one to second-guess himself and didn't consider the ramifications or the pros and cons. His decision made, he bolted from the grass to the side, which surprised one of the food-humans who'd crept closer. The two-leg fired his rifle, but Thor had already closed the distance, his jaw open to rend the food's chest as he barreled into him.

But his teeth didn't pierce his flesh. The outer skin —"clothes" that humans could change at will—yielded to his jaws but not completely. His teeth didn't penetrate.

The food screamed and beat on his head with his rifle butt, and the animal increased the pressure. His jaw began to cramp and the bone splinter from the other food was pushed deeper into his jaw, but he refused to give up. This wasn't right, and he didn't understand it. The food's struggles weakened but it was still alive, and more food-humans now rushed toward them.

He could feel the food's ribs creak. Well, if his teeth couldn't rip the man's lungs out, maybe he could crush them. He planted his forepaws on either side of the gurgling man's waist and, with a super-effort, bit down. The ribs cracked and the chest caved in.

The two-leg pawed weakly at his attacker's head as two more food humans rounded a large bush. Their eyes grew huge, but they didn't hesitate and raised their rifles. Thor couldn't savor his kill. He bolted forward and put the bush between them again to gain him a moment.

The two men rounded the bush from his right, so he went left. He circled in five tight bounds and his paws struggled to give him purchase as he caught up to the two who continued to pursue him—only he was much quicker.

He leapt onto the trailing food-human and his jaws snapped closed on the man's neck. This time, his fangs penetrated. One slid between the neck vertebrae and sliced the spinal cord in two as he rode it down. The food was dead before he landed. He gathered his feet and leapt again as the lead human spun, his mouth hanging open in surprise and fear.

Thor bit down on the human's thigh and expected to break the femur but once again, he couldn't penetrate. This time, the man's leg wasn't yielding, though, but hard. His teeth slid off as the two-leg fired his rifle and one round scored his back.

He began to lose his grip, and he knew that could be the end of him. If the human had more distance, he could fire his metal stick until it killed him.

The man scooted back when he tried to shift his grip, but his leg passed beneath Thor. In desperation, he bit again and this time, his fangs found flesh on the lower leg.

Acting instinctively, he began to run with the limb in his jaws. Both leg bones snapped, but it held together and he dragged the food-human over the ground. The man's body bounced off rocks and trees—and if Thor aimed at those rocks and trees, well, one had to do what one had to do.

The human cried out but each jolt weakened it as the animal raced away from the other food-humans. When the next impact against a large, jutting rock barely elicited a grunt, he slowed to a stop. He'd dragged the food some distance away and could still hear the others, but he had a few moments.

First things first. The food barely moved, his face covered in blood, dirt, and debris. One bite ended his misery.

Thor didn't take time to revel in the kill. He was confused. Two of the food-humans had resisted his bite, something that had never happened before.

He pawed at the food's thigh. There was something hard under the clothing. That wasn't the same where his fangs had penetrated farther down on the leg. He then pawed the food's torso. The clothes there were thicker and slightly yielding.

Thor took a tentative bite of the torso. His teeth didn't penetrate, and all it did was drive the annoying splinter of bone even farther into his gums.

Still confused, he sat on his haunches and cocked his head as he contemplated the situation. Soft but impenetrable in some places, hard in others, and nothing unusual covering the rest of the body.

Finally, something tickled his memory and he recalled being with Charles before they went into the Zoo. The three humans put extra clothes on and strapped them to their bodies before they left. It hadn't registered with him at the time, but now that he thought of it, Charles had been bit by various animals and not been hurt—bit in the same areas he'd playfully tussled with the man earlier. Those were areas where Thor knew if he'd wanted to, he could have bit and penetrated.

There was only one explanation. The extra clothing somehow gave protection even against his jaws. He didn't know how or why, only that it did.

Thor took a moment to listen and test the air. There were four, maybe five more food-humans out there. He didn't know how many of them had this protection on. That didn't change his plan to kill them. It merely meant he had to be smarter about it.

The first one was easy. Thor's natural instinct would have been to simply charge forward and challenge whoever was there. He had realized that would be suicide, however, so he stalked forward carefully and took advantage of each rock, bush, and tree for concealment. Two of them murmured to each other a little farther ahead, and he was focused on them when the slightest rustle above caught his attention.

He looked up, saw one of them up in a tree, and mentally kicked himself. Of course they could climb. They were exactly like his little stick-thrower at Achille's home, only bigger.

This food-human was focused on a cleared section beneath him, precisely where he had been headed. If he hadn't seen him, he would have been shot.

Thor didn't deal in what-ifs, though. He dealt with the present. Now that he knew where this food was and where he was looking, the advantage was his. He crept silently up behind the human and, as he'd contemplated doing with his diminutive stick-thrower, he leapt, clamped his jaws on the food's waist, and dragged him from the tree. The man landed on his head and both his skull and neck cracked. There was no need to even deliver the killing blow.

Shouts reached him, but he melted into the bush once again. He'd thought he'd located each of the food, but the one in the tree had been a surprise. It reminded him that he needed to be sure there were no other surprises out there.

He could sense Achille in the tall grass. His friend wasn't moving, but he didn't smell of death.

Two of the food were directly ahead, probably within a clump of bushes. The area around them was clear, which meant he would have to cross open ground to reach them. Another stretched prone in a small depression in the ground and had covered himself with leaves as he laid in wait. The final one had retreated to their main camp.

Thor considered killing the one near their camp first, but he wasn't a threat at the moment, while Achille was in danger from these three. Until he decided how to deal with the two who were together, he could kill the lone two-leg.

He circled quietly while his senses strained to locate another food-human he might have missed. As he approached the one in the depression, he couldn't detect anything else and was reassured that the man was alone.

When he positioned himself behind the one on the ground, he realized it was in a direct line of sight to the other two. He stood stock still and tried to locate them, the only thing moving being his tongue as it worried at the splinter of bone stuck in his gum.

The leaves covering the one in front of him stirred and Thor almost lunged forward, but the food-human had merely adjusted his position. The animal's lip rose in disdain. The man couldn't even freeze when his life depended on it. Not for the first time, he wondered how humans seemed not only to persevere, but to enforce their will on all other life.

What he couldn't tell was if this food-human wore the protective clothing. He knew exactly where it was but he couldn't see it, and his sense of smell was not attuned to this type of clothing.

He'd have to target the head.

Thor reached the man in three bounds, landed on his back, and clamped down on the neck to jerk the body free of its leafy covering. Two fangs penetrated but the rest were caught in the thick clothing around the base of the neck. He tried to move his hold, but the food struggled and his shifting weight kept him off balance. The two-leg uttered a shrill string of noise as he grappled and his hands clawed at his attacker's nose. Thor backed away and dragged his quarry with him when one of the others stood tall and fired at him.

One round, then a second struck the food in his jaws. The first thunked into the human's torso and he redoubled his fight to free himself. The second penetrated the food's head, exploded it, and made Thor flinch and drop the body.

Instinct told him that running would only present a target, so he did the only thing he could. He charged with a vicious snarl and hoped to make this human flinch.

Instead, the two-leg smiled widely with the look of a hunter before he stepped forward and aimed calmly at his attacker.

His attempt to rattle the food-human had obviously failed, and he could only hope that he could survive being wounded long enough to reach his target. A shot rang out, but instead of Thor feeling the lance of fire, the human dropped his rifle and raised his hand to his throat. The gloating look of victory had been replaced by one of surprise as he sank to his knees.

Behind the food, the second one stood and cried out as he reached toward his comrade. Thor didn't stop. He hurdled over the first as the second raised his rifle. His front paws caught him in the chest and hurled him onto his back.

The man's face twisted in anger, he cried, "Abiku," as he tried to bring his rifle to bear. He wore the thick clothing, but his face was bare. Thor bit down and ripped his quarry's jaw off. The food-human screamed and blood and tissue sprayed Thor in the face. One hand swung wildly.

A lucky punch connected to the side of his head and diverted his second bite, but that merely gained the man another three seconds of life. Thor would not be denied. The third bite savaged the human's throat.

He jumped free and his blood pounded while he searched for a new target. He noticed Achille, who stood near the tall grass where he'd been wounded, and from the food's camp, he could hear running feet moving away. Thor was in hunt mode, and he didn't give his friend-human another thought as he burst into a ground-covering race to close the distance with the fleeing food-human.

The camp was in the river bottom where the forest was thick. He had to slow considerably but the food had the same problem as he crashed through the vegetation in a mad rush. The man entered the camp and snatched a machete before he turned to face his oncoming doom.

Thor entered the camp and slowed, his eyes laser-focused on the food-human who stood trembling at the far side of the camp. He bristled his neck mane and started a slow, deliberate stalk forward while a low growl rose from deep inside as he advanced.

The last food gulped, stared at the apparition from hell with blood dripping from his fangs, and lost its nerve. He turned to run and the machete slid from nerveless fingers.

The stupid move hastened the very fate he'd hoped to avoid.

Thor rushed forward, head-butted the running food, and thrust him off his feet and onto his face. The man blubbered in fear and his hands scrabbled at the dirt in an effort to escape. He kept one paw planted on the two-leg's back to pin him in place.

Some of his bloodlust faded now that the danger was over. For a moment, he contemplated releasing this one. But humans were never alone. They always moved in packs. If this one was allowed to leave, it would bring others and that would be a threat to Achille.

Without the same burning rage as before, he bit down once on the food-human's neck and broke it cleanly. He stood and looked at the body and his stomach rumbled, making itself known now that the threat was gone.

Thor turned his head to look in the direction of Achille but his stomach rumbled again and refused to be ignored. He had used significant energy during the fight, and he hadn't had much to eat that morning. After everything he'd accomplished, he needed food.

He looked at the body. This was food and had been hard-earned.

For the second time since he'd arrived in his new home, he settled down to feed on his kill.

CHAPTER EIGHT

Achille

The ranger emerged from his hiding place in the grass in time to see Thor leave a prone body and charge the militiaman. The dog definitely wouldn't make it. The enemy stood cool and collected and aimed at his attacker. Achille acted instinctively, raised his FN, and snapped off a quick shot, hoping to distract the man long enough for Thor to reach him.

Luck shone on him, however, and Achille, who was a moderate marksman at best, struck the man in the neck. The militiaman sank to his knees with his hand to his throat.

Thor was like a missile and leapt over the dying man to catch a second, who had stepped out of his cover. The big dog bowled the man over and thrust him clear of the bushes.

"No!" Achille called, but the dog was in full frenzy. He bit down on the man's face and with bunched shoulders, tore the man's jaw off. The ranger took a step forward, shocked by the sheer primeval violence the dog displayed. He called for him to stop again, but as the man struggled, Thor sank his teeth into his throat and pulled most of it out. Blood sprayed into the air, a brilliant scarlet that caught the sun's rays.

Achille fell on his ass and his stomach threatened to revolt. He'd seen dead people before. His first was a poacher who had hunted lions, but the lions had turned the tables and he became the hunted. The ranger had gathered the scraps the lions left and delivered them to the man's wife in a village outside the park.

The second had been a victim of baboons but he never found out who the man was. The third had been bitten in half by a hippo when he'd paddled too close. Achille had helped fish the legs and pelvis out of the river.

Then there has been the firefight with the BOHICA Warriors with the kidnappers. People had been shot and he'd seen the bodies afterward.

But this had been the first time he's seen such a violent death as it occurred and he was shaken. It was…it was beyond comprehension.

And he was afraid of Thor.

He needed to hide, sure the dog would attack him next, but the animal sprinted in the other direction with a sense of purpose.

Achille's heart pounded. He knew he should go out there to see if anyone was still alive. The man he shot might be. It was his duty as a sworn officer of the country but he couldn't. He was too shaken.

Instead, he pushed farther into the grass and past the first dead militiaman, his right leg barely functional. It was swelling, and he knew he needed to slit the pants leg and take a look but the effort seemed too difficult. He wasn't bleeding out and that was good enough for the moment. He lay back and tried to make sense of what had happened.

On the one hand, he knew Thor had saved his life. The militiaman—mercenary, bandit, whatever these people were—had been about to kill him. His accent suggested that he came from outside Benin, but there were many tribes and nations in West Africa. Wherever he was from, there had been no mistaking his intent when he raised his rifle to cut Achille down.

On the other hand, however, Thor...

He didn't want to think about what he'd seen, but it was ingrained in his mind. It was something he would most likely never forget, and there was no way he could fool himself and regard Thor as only a dog any longer.

The ranger stared at the blue sky visible through the tall grass. He'd leave this death site when he could. He only needed to rest for a few minutes.

He awoke with a start and realized that the shadows were lengthening. Somehow, he'd fallen asleep. He sat up, wondering what had woken him, then clutched his leg and bit back a cry. It had swollen even more while he was out and now stretched his pants leg tight. He unbuckled his belt and tried to pull the pants down, but they were stuck on his leg by coagulated blood and his attempt shot lances of pain that reverberated to the top of his head.

Then, he heard a snap of a broken stick.

Instinctively, he froze and wished he could fade into nothingness. He didn't know what he feared more—Thor or one of the militiamen.

His FN was beside him and he inched his hand centimeter-by-centimeter to retrieve it before he raised it quickly and aimed at the tunnel he'd created in the grass. He had a very limited arc of vision beyond the vegetation, but that could be to his advantage. Someone walking outside would have to look in to see him.

A shadow crossed the opening, and Achille raised the rifle to his shoulder. A moment later, Thor rushed inside. He almost pulled the trigger, and for a fraction of a second, Thor's eyes flared red as he stopped at the opening, his body still.

I can still do it, he told himself. *One shot.*

"No," he said aloud. "You saved me."

With an extreme force of will, he laid his FN down beside him, ready for whatever might happen.

The second the rifle was on the ground, Thor rushed in with his mouth open as he crashed into Achille. Pain almost overwhelmed him and his leg screamed a protest. He grasped the animal by the ruff and tried to hold the jaws away. Thor was too strong, though, and he pushed in relentlessly…to cover him with sloppy licks with his huge blue tongue.

"Stop, stop," Achille said as Thor, in his eagerness, now stepped on his leg.

He might not be trying to eat him, but the dog might kill him in his eagerness.

Achille surveyed the camp and refused to look at the pile of clothing and body armor that lay in a bloody heap at one end. One of the boots was half-eaten, and that was all he wanted to see. But he still had a job to do and he couldn't let a squeamish stomach get in the way.

The camp was well-hidden from overhead surveillance. Military-style netting was held up by lines attached to the trees. The gear in the camp was new and first-rate, far better than what local poachers could afford.

If he had any lingering thoughts that these could be locals, those were destroyed by the large pile of ivory and six rhino horns loaded on pallets. He had no idea how they brought all this in—and more pertinently, how they expected to get it out—but all signs indicated that this was a major operation.

Achille had seen five bodies if he included the lunch at the side of the camp. They all wore the same uniform which, while military in style, matched none of the regional militaries. They could be a militia group as he'd first surmised, and they could be one of the local warlord troops, but both rarely showed such uniformity. His guess now was that these were corporate mercenaries.

But why were they poaching? They usually protected commercial interests such as pipelines, or they intimated local villages in order to push through favorable rights to resources. Benin wasn't rich in the resources the corporations wanted, however, except in wildlife, but what would the corporations want with them? It made no sense.

Militias and warlords often poached to help buy more weapons and to feed their soldiers. This group didn't seem to be one that needed to supplement their income.

But his eyes didn't lie. They were poaching. Not only that, this camp was better outfitted than it should be for five mercs. It was designed to accommodate far greater numbers. Those Thor had killed were holding the fort down, nothing more, and that meant there were others out there poaching animals.

If that were the case, they would be none too pleased that their comrades had been killed—and one eaten.

As if on cue, Thor walked over to that one, flopped down with the half-eaten boot between his front paws, and began to chew on it. Achille started to call him off but what was the use? He'd been careful to leave no trace that he'd been in the camp, but it would be impossible for him to clean Thor's sign. Maybe they'd think it was lions, even if his pawprints didn't match that of the big cats.

Baboons hooted in the distance. Achille jerked his head up and scanned the dense forest. They were reasonably far off, at least two kilometers. Maybe they'd seen a leopard… or maybe a returning hunting party. It was time for them to leave.

"Thor, come!" he said.

The…*dog*, he told himself again, bounded up, obviously pleased with himself. He sniffed the wound on Achille's leg again and gave it a few more licks. The ranger had slit his pants legs to relieve the pressure and he'd been surprised when Thor had licked the wound clean. He hadn't stopped him. Some old villagers swore by the healing properties of dog saliva. He wasn't so sure, but at least that had cleaned most of the dried blood.

Thor flopped at his feet and pawed at his jaws. He shook his head and whined.

"What's the matter, boy?"

In response, he opened his mouth wide and whined

again. Achille knelt, caught his lower jaw, and twisted Thor's head so he could see inside. The gums around the right upper jaw were inflamed. Forgetting that those jaws had recently killed at least five men, he reached in while Thor lay still. Carefully, he poked around the most swollen area and his prodding fingers felt something sharp.

"What do you have there, Thor?" he asked as he pulled at the object.

It came out easily, and once he held it closer to see what it was, he dropped it and shook his hand as if to be rid of the touch. It was a shard of bone, and he was very sure he knew what kind of bone.

Thor yipped and licked his hand.

It took an effort of will to bend, pick the piece of bone up again, and toss it into the bushes. Whoever might be coming didn't need to see that. At the thought, he looked in the direction of the baboons again. It was long past time to go.

Achille had to reach his bike. The question, though, was how. The shortest route was cross-country, but he didn't know if he could make it. He took a step to test his leg and it almost buckled.

Thor cocked his head and looked at him with one ear erect while the shot one flopped to the side. He stepped close, put his head under the man's hand, and stood erect to take some of the pressure off him.

"You can tell I need help?" Achille asked, surprised.

He knew Thor was smart, but this?

Tentatively, he tried another step, and with Thor beside him, it was better. Still, was it good enough? Achille knew it wasn't. He couldn't make the trek. That left the long route, or he could continue on the trail leading away from the camp to the highway and cut back to the trail with his bike. It was farther but definitely more manageable.

The mercs knew about the trail, however. If a group of them approached the camp, he had to stay alert enough to see them first and find cover.

There was nothing more than to simply do it. He leaned on Thor, held one of his horns for stability, and lurched out of the camp.

The next eight hours were some of the toughest in Achille's life. His leg stiffened and each step was agony. He knew he was lucky that no one came down the trail and wasn't sure he could have gotten off it and under cover.

It came as something of a surprise when they reached the highway. One minute, they were on the trail and seemingly in the next, they trudged down the paved road. Thor supported him loyally as they made their way slowly forward. Twice, they had to leave and crouch alongside the road as trucks drove past, but the weak headlights failed to pick them up. Each time, it had needed a superhuman effort to stand and resume his walk.

Somewhere along the way, Achille lost his pack. That held their food and water, which made matters worse. If his FN hadn't been slung on his back, he would have lost that too.

He never would have made it to the bike if it weren't for Thor. It wasn't only the weight the dog bore, but he forced him off the road when they reached the trail where his bike was hidden. Otherwise, he'd have walked on past without a thought.

Knowing they'd made it this far gave Achille a jolt of

energy. He was able to drag his bicycle out of hiding and to the side of the road. He couldn't swing his left leg over, though, so he had to stand on his left and swing his right over.

As soon as he tried to pedal, he crashed. Thor licked his face as he tried to clamber to his feet. He squatted, or at least tried to squat. His left leg wouldn't bend. In the dark, he couldn't see it and he was glad of that. He was afraid he'd see the signs of infection. People had been known to die in the bush from a simple scrape, and this was a bullet wound.

"It's okay, boy. I can pedal with one leg."

He left his left leg straight and pushed down with his right. The bike moved forward but the right pedal didn't make it back to the top and he had to step off to keep upright.

"Let's try it again."

Achille took a deep breath and pushed down harder. This time, the bicycle moved farther, enough that the pedal returned to a position where he could push down again. Achille kept this up for about five minutes and covered six or seven hundred meters before his battered body could take no more. He coasted to a stop and fell on his side. His right leg cramped and his lungs struggled to pull oxygen in.

"Sorry, boy, but I don't think I can do this. I have to rest."

He dragged the bike to the side of the road and sat there with one arm around Thor.

The big dog seemed content to stay with him, but Achille could feel the tension in him. He knew Thor was protecting him and alert for any danger.

If he needed a guardian angel, he wasn't a bad choice. With his arm around him, the ranger could feel the corded muscles. The animal was powerful enough to tear the head off one of the poachers.

Achille had come to grips with the carnage. It was what he'd planned, after all—to use Thor to protect the park. One of them had tried to kill him, and the rest...well, he had seen the ivory and he'd seen the rhinoceros horns. There were very few rhinos in the park, and those horns represented lost generations to come.

They got what was coming to them.

He gave Thor an affectionate tug, and the beast barely budged.

That gave him an idea—a farfetched idea, but one nonetheless.

The ranger felt around his waist where he'd looped the line. It was still there, to his relief. For all he knew, he could have lost it with his pack.

He unwound it and tied one end to the bicycle frame. He looped the other over Thor's back to see if there would be a reaction. The dog licked his forepaws and ignored the rope.

"I'm going to tie this around you, okay, Thor?" he said and leaned closer to him.

Thor heard his name and turned his head to lick his face.

Achille took that as assent and he ran the rope around his chest and over his neck once more before he tied it off behind the base of his horns. Thor lowered his head and tried to sniff the rope, but he didn't fight it.

"Let's try it," he said and stood the bicycle up.

Thor stood as well, ready to move on.

He mounted, then said, "Go!"

The dog looked at him, the moonlight bright enough for Achille to see he was confused.

"Go!" he said again and pointed forward.

The dog stepped beside him and gave his hand a lick.

"No, I need you to pull me." He gave him a push.

Thor obediently stepped forward but stopped and looked back when he realized the man wasn't moving. He uttered a confused-sounding whine.

"Go," he said again and this time, pushed down on the right pedal.

With him moving, the animal walked forward and as Achille slowed, Thor took up the slack and jerked the bike forward. The abrupt movement caused the ranger to lose his balance and crash, which startled Thor.

He came back and licked the man's face as he made sounds Achille swore was him trying to speak.

Too tired, I guess. I'm imagining things.

It took four more failures before Thor, as if a light switch had turned on, seemed to understand. He pulled the bicycle while Achille struggled to maintain balance. There were two more accidents while the two felt out the process, but twenty minutes after tying his dog to the bike, they mushed along well enough to make the Iditarod proud.

The sun on his face woke Achille, and he groaned. The night had been a blur and evidently, also a failure. He'd fallen somewhere and never managed to stand. A stick struck him on his nose and he opened his eyes. Above him, a red-bellied monkey peered down from a tree.

"Just like Mr. Ogbé," Achille muttered. "What is with you guys and sticks?"

He turned his head. Thor was asleep next to him, still with the rope around him. Beyond him was a building—

"We made it!" he said and bounded to his feet. "You did it!"

They were on the ground in front of his station. Thor had brought them home.

Achille moved to untie the dog, and a twinge in his leg stopped him. Then, he realized it was merely a twinge, not the pain he would have expected. He stooped to look at his leg. The bullet holes were there—one entry and one exit wound—but they were closing, and instead of being an angry red with weeping pus, they were pink and dry. He poked the front wound. It hurt but not like it should.

Carefully, he flexed his leg. Scar tissue pulled and it hurt, but there was no way scar tissue could form that fast.

"Is it true?" he asked Thor. "Is dog saliva really that effective?"

The dog opened one eye and gave him a long look before he rolled over and went back to sleep.

CHAPTER NINE

Thor

They were going out again at last. Thor jumped up and down in his excitement.

His own wounds had healed within a day, but Achille's had taken longer. Thor couldn't smell any contagion in the wound, but the human limped around the station and never ventured far.

On the second day home, the man had tied him in one of the sheds and said, "Stay!" He didn't like it and even more so when other humans arrived in one of their "cars." He had developed a very protective attitude over Achille and he almost rushed out to defend him, but he greeted the three men and escorted them into the station.

He waited anxiously, only held back by that stay. Unable to settle, he stood on his hind legs and looked out of the window, whining quietly. At last, the other humans left and as Achille started to walk over to him, he couldn't wait any longer. He broke the rope as if it weren't there and barreled through the door. In his exuberance, he reached the man in three bounds and almost knocked his friend to the ground in his eagerness to check him over.

Achille laughed and pushed him back, and Thor couldn't smell any new hurt on him. Evidently, the humans who'd come were not food but friends.

Finally, though, after six days, the ranger had slung his rifle, put food and water in his pack, and called for Thor to follow. He'd beaten him to the punch, however. Once he saw him put the food into the pack, he had run down the dirt road and braved the little two-leg to where he now jumped up and down as he waited for his friend to reach him.

"Getting bored here, Thor? I guess it's time for a little trek. I want you to see something," Achille said.

Instead of turning to the right as they'd done before, the man crossed the road and into the bush on the other side. This was new territory for Thor, and he sniffed the air and cataloged every scent.

Within an hour, there were new smells. Not new to Thor but new to this place—humans, and many of them, along with smoke and the nasty-smelling water they fed their cars. For a moment, Thor wondered if they would return to the Zoo and his ears perked up with the hope he would see Charles. But his internal compass kicked in and he remembered they were far from the Zoo, and the familiar human smells weren't accompanied by the vibrant and rich scents of the jungle itself.

Curious, he began to pick up the pace, but Achille snagged one of his horns and pulled him back.

"Heel," he said, one of the sounds that he still didn't

understand. Achille often said it, but he never showed him what it meant.

Whatever heel meant, the meaning of the hand grasping his horn was clear. He wanted him close.

That must mean that those humans were food, too. Achille wanted him to protect him. Thor uttered a soft growl and his lips lifted off his teeth. He took a step forward to put his body between his friend and the food ahead.

The ranger pushed ahead and his knee caught Thor in the side so it became difficult for him to keep up and keep between the man and the others.

"What's a matter with you, Thor?" the man said. "Don't keep tripping me."

They continued this dance with Achille pushing and the dog maneuvering. He didn't understand what his human was doing, but he would make sure his friend was not hurt.

Finally, as they came to a clearing in the trees, Achille forced him to his belly.

"Look out there, Thor," he said and pointed across the opening.

It was a human hive. Not like where Charles, Booker, and Roo lived outside the Zoo, but there was no mistaking the homes the humans had built.

Then, something caught his attention and he would have popped up on his hind legs to look had Achille not pulled him down. He'd heard a squeal like one of the pseudo-gazelles being caught. It looked like two of the humans were chasing each other. More than that, they were miniature humans—not like the small two-leg in the trees but real humans, complete with clothes.

"Down, Thor. I don't want you to be seen."

One of the small humans caught the other, and Thor expected to see the kill. Instead, as soon as it touched the other, it turned and ran the other way, laughing as the original target became the hunter.

Human cubs, Thor realized. He'd never seen the young of the humans, and it had never dawned on him that they had them. But there was no other explanation.

Achille pulled his head over so he could look into Thor's eyes.

"Thor, those over there, they are friends. They are not the enemy."

Friends?

"Do you understand? Friends. Not poachers."

Most of what Achille said was lost on him, the sounds meaning no more and maybe even less than that of the crickets that sang in the grass. But he understood friends.

Those humans out there were not food. They were friends. Thor didn't really know how to differentiate between the two, but it was good enough if Achille said so. He wouldn't eat them.

"Friends," he said, or at least tried to. He hadn't mastered the many sounds a human throat made, and even he could tell he wasn't close.

Achille looked surprised, however, and asked, "Did you just try to talk to me?"

But Thor's attention was already back on the small humans—the cubs. Something in him wanted to rush forward and play like he'd done with Charles.

They laid at the edge of the forest for quite some time—how long, he didn't know. His inner clock was now short-time and long-time. At last, Achille tugged at his horn and they edged away before they stood and headed home.

He took one last long draught of air, savored the scent, and wondered if he would ever be able to play with a human cub.

CHAPTER TEN

Achille

The trip to the village had gone well, Achille thought. Thor seemed to understand that they were not poachers. Well, some of them probably were, but that was beside the point. If he unleashed the animal, he didn't want there to be a bloodbath among the innocent.

He scratched behind Thor's ear as they headed to the station. It was hard to fathom that this animal that padded beside him was the same demon that had killed at least five poachers…and eaten one of them.

Am I doing the right thing?

The ranger hadn't been responsible for the deaths in the bush, at least not directly. Well, maybe he was, but he hadn't ordered Thor to kill. The dog had merely tried to protect him, and while he was grateful for that and wouldn't change a thing, he wasn't sure he could control him if it came to that. He'd seen the wild fury when he had killed.

Achille hadn't stepped over the line yet. If he took Thor

out specifically to hunt poachers, he indisputably would. He'd step into a deep void, one from which there was no return.

Thor twisted his head to lick his hand. The dog had kept close tabs on him since the fight with the poachers. For the hundredth time, he wondered if there was something to the old grannies' tales about dog saliva. His leg shouldn't be this healed. It was a little sore after the walk to the village and back, but it was fully functional with no sign of infection.

He didn't completely buy into the notion, but if he was shot again, he would definitely get Thor to lick the wound.

Of course, he hoped it would never come to that. Ranger Chief Modeste Loko, his boss, had told him to take a month off to heal and he'd assigned Josaphat Yassou, a young ranger made from the same mold as Achille, to keep tabs on the area. Achille had told him that there were more out there, but Loko wanted that confirmed before he reported up his chain. If these poachers had friends on high, his chief would have to navigate tricky waters if he started handing out accusations.

Glad it's him and not me, Achille thought as the two reached the station. *There's no way I could handle the politics.*

Magical dog spit or not, his leg protested as he climbed the steps and into the station. He lowered himself gratefully into his ancient but still serviceable overstuffed chair he'd scrounged during one of his semi-annual trips to headquarters in Contonou.

Thor flopped on the floor at his feet, and within moments, he was snoring.

Achille sat for several minutes and simply watched the

dog. He still had three weeks left before Loko expected him back on duty. That was three more weeks in which to decide if he would attempt to turn Thor into a weapon.

Two days later, Achille was out in the bush with Thor, unable to merely sit back at the station. The dog seemed happy to be out as well and bounded from one clod of dirt to a clump of grass and on to another clod like an overgrown horned puppy.

After a couple of hours and less than four kilometers from the station, he saw a rhinoceros. The scarred ear identified him as Ipanilaya, or Bully, as this old bull was apt to chase away others. Achille hadn't seen him in over a year —his territory was farther north, closer to the Niger River —and it gave him a warm feeling to know the big old guy hadn't fallen prey to poachers.

He remained carefully downwind and out beyond the rhino's poor eyesight, content to watch him forage with an egret perched on his back, ready to pounce on any small creature disturbed by the rhino's progress. This was why he was a ranger. With all the losses in his life, this was what made it all worthwhile. He was blessed to be a part of this grand panoply.

Thor's soft growl snapped him from his reverie and he reacted instantly and caught his horn to keep him from advancing on the rhino. But the dog's attention was to the right of the beast and on something out of sight.

Not much other than man could threaten a rhino, not that Thor's countenance meant there was a human in that direction. But while Achille knew in his heart that he was anthropomorphizing his dog, he still wanted to believe that he had adopted his own protective nature over the park and the animals in it. Regardless, whatever had alerted him deserved an investigation.

Achille melted into the bush in the direction from which they'd come and pulled hard on Thor's tail until he followed. They circled and stopped every twenty meters or so to listen and watch. As the sun heated up, many of the small animals took shelter and it seemed unnaturally quiet.

It took an hour in which Achille's nerves were almost frayed to breaking point, but at last he saw what he had searched for. Boot prints were visible in the dirt. A single set of military boots had made them and within the morning. He knelt and stared ahead but he couldn't discern any movement.

One thing was almost certain, however. Whoever it was, he'd watched the rhino as well. It was one person and probably male. That eliminated the possibility that it might be a photographer. Not the male part—many who came into the park were foreign women. But neither they nor the male photographers went out alone. They had guides and the legitimate guides would have checked in at the station.

No, this was a poacher. Achille felt it in his gut.

So, now what? he wondered and glanced at Thor.

The dog's nostrils flared as he tested the air. There was none of the reaction from before, which suggested that the poacher was no longer nearby.

Not that Achille believed the man had abandoned the rhino. A local villager out for bush meat or looking for honey would have avoided the big animal and moved out of its way. No, this man wanted Ipanilaya.

Anger flared when he thought of the old rhino being killed simply for his horn. It would be made into dagger handles for Yemini princes or to be ground up so rich Chinese businessmen could eat it and get their dicks hard.

"Viagra's cheaper," he muttered to himself.

The poacher wouldn't kill Ipanilaya right now, he was sure. He'd wait until dusk before shooting the beast so he'd have time to cut the horn off undisturbed. Achille had to make sure he was there to stop him. The best way to do that would be to follow the rhino until the poacher revealed himself.

He looked at Thor, who still quested the air. Achille had thought he'd have three weeks before he decided if he would go through with this crazy plan or not.

Instead, the time was now.

CHAPTER ELEVEN

Thor

He stared intently in the direction of the setting sun and ignored the rhinoceros that stood thirty meters away. His ears were on a swivel to discern the slightest tread of food approaching.

Or enemy, as Achille called not-friends. Thor hadn't made the connection before today, but he was sure of it. Still, not-friends would always be food to him.

"You hear something?" Achille whispered to him when he noted his body-language. "Is he here?"

The two had shadowed the rhino all day, ever since they found sign that someone else had taken an interest in the beast as well. Thor had picked up the food's scent long before Achille had found the tracks. He didn't know why his friend hadn't tried to track the food, but he'd followed and quested constantly for the human.

Now, with the unmistakable tread of someone stalking, he realized that Achille had been right. When Thor had run with his pack in the Zoo, they often worked together to surround and herd the pseudo-gazelles to where others in the pack were lying in wait, which made an easy kill. There might only be two in his current pack, but Achille had planned it perfectly. The food would emerge very close to them.

Thor was bigger and stronger than his companion, but his human friend had now shown why he was the alpha. He had challenged the alpha in his old pack, but he was content to let the man guide their actions.

"Food," he tried to say, but what emerged from his jaws didn't sound at all like it did when the humans made the sound.

"Sshh," Achille said and slid his hand around his muzzle.

He wanted to stalk forward but remained where he was, tracked the sounds of the approaching two-leg, and waited for him to become visible. He knew by now that humans didn't have his sense of smell, but if he could see the food-human, Achille would take action, either with his rifle or by sending him to attack.

As the thought occurred, he glanced quickly at the ranger, suddenly fearful that his friend would take the kill shot. He wanted it himself and he didn't want him to deprive him of the kill. But Achille was the alpha, so he would make the decision.

Finally, matters came to a head. The food-human stepped into sight, his attention focused on the rhino. He'd been careful to stay downwind, but each step brought him closer to the two of them.

"Mauser M 98 Magnum firing the .416 Rigby. He's no

hungry villager but a professional big game poacher," Achille muttered quietly.

Thor didn't understand any of that, but he could feel the venom in the ranger's voice. If he hadn't been sure if the human was food or not before, that cemented it.

The rhino was oblivious to the approaching threat, and Thor's excitement rose. Because Achille was so happy with the somewhat boring animals in the park and he wanted to keep the man happy, he'd begun to feel like it was his job to protect them.

But there was also the thrill of the hunt, especially when hunting a food-human who could kill him. Thor had seen enough of his Zoo brethren—some much, much larger than him—that the humans killed. He knew that could be his fate if he wasn't good enough.

But that didn't dissuade him. It only heightened the rush.

Achille pulled Thor's head to him until their eyes were only centimeters apart. He sensed that the man was torn and that he had to make a decision, although he didn't understand why. To him, there was only one possible course of action.

Finally, the ranger nodded, released him, and simply said, "Kill."

CHAPTER TWELVE

Achille

"No, no, madame, I'm just a poor ranger. I can't afford that," Achille told the woman selling *yovo doko*. Her hand held the spoon full of batter expectantly over the hot oil.

"I tell you what, Mr Ranger-man. You being what you are, if you can tell me what's going on up there in the park, I think I can give you a better price."

"What do you mean, madame?" he asked and his heart thudded painfully.

Do they know what we've been doing?

Over the past two weeks, he and Thor had killed three poachers, not including the five or more who were part of a bigger plan, nor the two Thor had killed on his own. That was at least ten poachers or mercenaries dead, all in the space of three weeks. Did she suspect him?

Achille looked around and tried to plot an escape route. He thought he could get away from the overweight saleslady. His leg was completely healed by now and he felt fit. But then what?

Achille had told Thor to stay and rode his bicycle to RNEIE7 highway where he hitched a ride into Banikoara to stock up on necessities. Loko had called him to say that the truck he sent with supplies had broken down and it wouldn't be fixed for at least two weeks. This wasn't the first time it had happened, so he had to go to the closest market—a two-hour truck ride away—to restock the essentials.

Banikoara was not a big town, and if he ran, where would he go? He still had to catch a ride home.

"Don't play coy with me. I know you can't be scaring the tourists, no doubt. But I won't talk. You can trust me with a secret."

I couldn't trust you with the day of the week, he thought.

"I don't know what you mean, madame."

She smiled as she dropped the batter into the oil where it sputtered, evidently sure that he wouldn't be able to resist. And it was a good bet. Achille might not be able to resist, he knew. He was particularly fond of the local version of beignets—*yovo doko* even meant European pastry.

"The man-eater, man. The man-eater," she said.

Do they know about Thor? he wondered in alarm and his mind ripped away from the frying dough.

Thor had only eaten three of the poachers, but that qualified him for the title.

"Word is, one of those lions of yours is eating folk," she said with a conspiratorial whisper. "They hunt him and he eats them."

Achille felt a wave of relief wash over him for a moment, quickly followed by concern. Relief that no one knew about Thor but fear that he could be asked to cull a man-eating lion—when no lions were guilty of that.

Her eyes lit up as she caught him by the shirt and pulled him close.

"Only, I don't think it's a lion, no, no."

"Who...what do you think it is?"

"Oh, so there is something there, then," she said with a laugh. "But I think it's an orisha like Aja. A guardian of the forest. Paying back all those who abuse nature."

Many people in Benin—especially the Fon—while nominally Christian or Muslim, still believed in Vodun or what the foreigners call Voodoo. They didn't see why they couldn't believe in both religions. The orisha were spirits that controlled all aspects of life, and Aja was the spirit of the forest.

"Most of the people here, they be afraid now to go to the forest up there," she said. "Our witchdoctor, he be making *boucou* francs making *bocio,* you know."

Achille didn't believe in Vodun—for the most part—and he'd rather trust his FN than a carved wooden *bocio* for protection in the bush. But he'd learned long ago not to be critical of those who did believe.

"I don't know if there's an orisha. Maybe yes. Maybe no," Achille said. "But I've never seen one."

"That's because you be a guardian, too. Ol' Aja, she got no beef with you, Mr Ranger-man."

"If I see an orisha, I'll be the first to tell you, madame," he said with a forced laugh and hastened to change the subject. "But until then, how about one hundred francs for the *yovo doko?*"

Oh, my God," she said and clutched her heart, "I said a

better price, but not one to put me in the poorhouse. I couldn't go anything less than three hundred."

Achille had been surprised by the woman's questions and he knew he needed to consider what he could do with the rumor. But now, he had a bargain to make and those golden-fried pastries did look delicious.

CHAPTER THIRTEEN

Thor

His little two-leg had followed him up in the trees as Thor trotted through the bush but for once, hadn't thrown anything at him. When he crossed a stream, however, the animal quit pacing him. He stopped and looked back, but the two-leg simply perched on a branch and watched him silently.

Achille had told him to stay that morning before he left and he had…kind of. He hadn't followed his friend, at least. But how far did stay allow him to go?

Thor decided that it allowed him to go back to the place where the young humans were. He was curious about them and he had nothing else to do with Achille gone. He might as well satisfy his curiosity.

Finding the place was easy. He had a firm grasp of location and could navigate anywhere after he'd been there once. Unlike the Zoo, this place didn't change on a daily basis, which made it even easier.

There were fewer animals the closer he got to the

humans. Patches of ground had been cleared of the native vegetation and planted in smooth, even rows, which almost hurt his sensibilities after the chaos of the Zoo and the haphazard patterns around Achille's home.

Twice, smaller hornless versions of what looked like him ran out to challenge his passage. One barked twice, thought better of it, and slunk away, his tail between his legs. Another one, mangy and ragged, maintained a tirade of barking and remained a little ahead of him while he passed the field. It somehow reminded him of the small two-leg—all bluster but never straying too close.

Thor could have reached the little guy in one pounce, but it wouldn't be worth the effort. It would only make an appetizer, but the real reason he didn't was because he rather admired the animal's spunk.

As he moved closer to his destination, he began to identify sounds. He couldn't understand them, but some of them had a sense of urgency about them. More than a little curious, he wondered what that meant but his attention was drawn by a cry off to his left.

He stopped and swung his head from side to side between the direction of the cry and the place ahead with the human friends. The cry could be any number of animals, and his destination was the human place. He dismissed the cry and began to trot ahead when the wind shifted and brought him the scent of a human intermixed with the sharp, pungent scent of something different. He recalled that Achille had called it a hyena. In this case, several of them, he realized quickly.

Thor spun on his hind legs, reoriented, and raced away. A howl burst from his chest and reverberated through the bush. The hyenas smelled of the hunt and the human smelled of fear.

It was an easy equation. The human was friend because Achille said so. The hyenas were not. The ranger had made it clear that he was not supposed to hunt any of the animals around them, so they weren't food and he had no animosity toward them. But they weren't friend, either.

He covered the ground between them quickly and barreled into one of the odd areas of plants. In the middle of the field was a single small tree. A young human was perched in the tree while seven hyenas paced around it. Another single animal attempted to reach the crying human, who had drawn her legs up in an effort to keep out of reach.

It jumped and bit the human's foot, but all it was rewarded with was a "shoe." The human screamed and tried to climb higher and the tree leaned dangerously.

Like an avenging angel, Thor charged across the field to scatter the seven scavengers. The one focused on the human hadn't even noticed his approach when he hammered into its shoulder and clamped his jaws on its neck.

The hyena yelped and jumped back, dragging him with it. His jaws were immensely powerful, and he was surprised that he hadn't killed the animal.

Its shrill cries as it struggled to free itself matched those of the human. Its own jaws snapped shut perilously close to his front paw.

He had no inherent desire to kill it and anyway, it wasn't food. As it merely attempted to escape, he released it, and it scrambled across the field to where the others waited for it.

The human was still crying so Thor turned away from the hyenas and stepped under the tree. He stood on his hind legs and stretched his full length with his forepaws on the trunk of the tree, which unfortunately bent over even more while the human shrieked in fear.

"Friend." Thor made the sound, or rather tried to. What came out was nothing close to it. The human shouted different sounds that he didn't understand.

What he did understand was that the youngster was afraid. In an attempt to reassure it, he stretched farther and licked its naked foot.

He soon realized that it had not been a good move.

The human jerked up higher and the tree began to crack under their combined weight. Thor immediately dropped to all fours.

As he contemplated what to do next, his ears detected movement. He turned and saw that the hyenas had returned. Eight of them now attempted to surround the two of them.

Thor had seen this before in the Zoo and he'd even participated in it. His pack often drove off larger, more powerful predators from their kill. He was more than powerful enough to hold off a single hyena, but eight?

It looked like he'd find out.

The human no longer screamed but she cried softly above him. He put her out of his mind. Eight hyenas could kill him and once he was disposed of, they'd kill the young human. He had to concentrate.

As the beasts began to close in, Thor rapped his horns

against the trunk of the tree which made the human cry out again. He raised his head and howled as he expanded his ruff. The hyenas startled but they quickly regained their composure and renewed their determined advance.

Thor didn't want to kill any of them, but they were determined to press their attack. Given a friend and not-friend, he had no choice.

If he was not overmatched, of course.

One of the hyenas darted in and its teeth snapped. Thor wheeled to meet it and it scampered back while another lunged forward to bite his exposed flank. Except this wasn't his first rodeo. He'd expected this, and quicker than the animal could have imagined, he wheeled with his head down and caught it with his horns. With one flick of his massive neck, the hyena was airborne, its side punctured.

It screamed piteously as it careened away and landed hard on its side where it lay inert and its lungs struggled to breathe. Within a moment, all movement ceased.

The remaining attackers stopped and looked at each other for a moment before an unseen command sent them forward to meet him. Thor waited and tried to choose the right target. A big female seemed to be the alpha, so he charged her. She turned to flee as the others closed in to protect her, but she was too slow. He bit down on her weak hindquarters before he released her quickly and faced the remainder of the pack. The alpha squealed in pain and used her front legs to drag herself clear.

The other hyenas, now six of them, surrounded him. They feinted and darted in and out but at this range, he couldn't target any specific one before the others closed in on him again.

He tried to come up with a plan when suddenly, all six alerted to something beyond the tree and the young human. Fearful of a ruse, he refused to look, but when human shouts sounded, the six hyenas scattered, left the dead one behind, and ignored the wounded alpha.

Thor turned to see seven humans armed with sticks and metal implements—not rifles, but some other human-type things. The two-legs sprinted across the field, brandished the sticks, and yelled at the top of their voices.

Thor sat and his tail thumped a welcome as they reached the young human. One reached up to rescue her while the others put themselves between him and the tree.

They yelled at him, their actions definitely aggressive.

"No! Friend," he wanted to tell them but once again, his jaw and tongue wouldn't cooperate.

The young human made more noises, and she pointed to the dead hyena. The older humans looked warily before they made excited noises. They were still aggressive but lowered their weapons slightly.

Not that they needed the sticks. They were friend-humans, not food.

Other sounds were exchanged and at last, they lowered their sticks hesitantly. Thor thought that was a sign and he started toward them. Immediately, the sticks were raised again.

It made him sad when he realized that they didn't know he was a friend. He wanted to see the young human up close, but the old ones would not let him near her.

He sat once again, his head cocked as he watched the wary two-legs. One of them made sounds at him, but he didn't understand. They used none of the same sounds as Charles or Achille.

Their fear was tangible and he understood it. The young human had almost been killed and they were on edge. It was time for him to go and let them calm again. Maybe another time, and with Achille, he could return.

Slowly so as to not alarm them, he turned and walked past the dead hyena and into the forest.

CHAPTER FOURTEEN

Achille

"What did this animal look like?" Achille asked the man.

"It wasn't an animal. I told you, it was Aja," the young girl interrupted defiantly.

He knew exactly what the animal looked like, but he had to make a pretense. Loko had called him on the DR the day before and asked him to look into reports of either a demon or an angel, depending on who described it, that had made an appearance in the village outside the park's boundary.

Somehow, Thor had made his way back to the village he'd shown him, and in the process, saved the young girl from hyenas. She now glared at him. The how and the why's were beyond him, but he had to somehow defuse the rumors.

It was bad enough with this village, where Thor was seen as the orisha guardian angel of the forest, Aja. Elsewhere, however, he was Abiku, the orisha demon who liked to eat people. There were reports of missing men, many more than the ones he and Thor had killed, and people refused to enter the park.

Which was fine with Achille. To him, even the legitimate tourists were a burden to bear. Their foreign dollars helped fund the park but if he had his way, the entire area would be off-limits to people.

"So, what did Aja look like?" he asked and directed the question to the young girl who could be no more than seven.

"She was gold-colored with white wings," she said. "She had two horns made of silver, and her eyes were red."

She got one right, at least.

"She saved me from the hyenas," she said with the conviction only the young could muster.

What was she doing out all alone? he wondered.

Animal life outside the park was more limited, but green mambas, baboons, lions, and yes, hyenas, were only some of the animals that did not respect park boundaries. A young girl like this would be easy prey for too many species.

And you would have been in a hyena's belly now if it weren't for Thor.

"And did you see this animal?" he asked the father before he changed it quickly to, "this Aja," when he saw fire about to erupt from the girl's eyes.

"Yes, I did."

"And what did you see?"

The man looked at the daughter, who still stared daggers at the ranger. He opened his mouth, closed it, and his brow furrowed as he considered his words before he said, "Just like Corine said."

The girl nodded her head in vindication.

Achille would clearly not get this man to naysay his daughter. He could understand that, too. But he would have to get the man off on his own and grill him. He needed to know if there was an accurate description of Thor floating out there.

Much of what was being reported was fantasy. There were reports of the Abiku killing in the southern part of the WAP, all the way to the Pendjari National Park and far beyond where Thor could ever go. Right now, there would be other rangers down there who interviewed people and hated every minute of chasing imaginary ghosts. Only Achille knew there was some truth to the rumors, at least up here.

Things were getting out of hand, and he wondered how much longer he could continue his mission. And why had Thor left the station area?

He'd taken no chances this time and tied him to his bed inside the building. The last thing he needed would be to have him race off to save someone else while he interviewed these villagers.

Achille asked a few more questions, barely listened to the answers, and pretended to take notes. He said he'd return and retrieved his bicycle.

"Don't you try to hunt Aja," the little girl ran up to him and said. "She protects the forest and all the animals."

"Don't worry about that. I won't," he said.

"Do you want me to escort you out?" the father said. "I mean, if the hyenas come back."

He knew the man wanted to give his description out of hearing of his daughter. Achille also knew he should hear him out, but he patted the FN slung across his back and said no. There really was no need to waste any more time.

This was all for show, anyway. He'd report the girl's description and maybe leave the horns out and stress the wings. Many superstitious people lived in the country, and this would be passed off as more of the crazies' imagination by the educated bureaucracy.

This time, however, the crazies were closer to the truth.

CHAPTER FIFTEEN

Thor

The elephants pulled the branches down from the treetops and dropped some on the ground so the little ones could feed. This was the same herd Thor had first met when the littlest one had made friends with him.

Achille, however, was content to stand far away and simply watch. Thor didn't understand. These were friends, not food.

And they knew the two were there. The largest had trumpeted when she saw them but after that, they'd been ignored. The herd made their way slowly to the water as they browsed and eventually, they passed out of view.

"Okay, Thor. Let's move on. We have those school children tomorrow, and now that I know where the herd is today, I hope I can find them in the morning."

Achille set off with Thor obediently at his side. This was the farthest they'd trekked since the man had tied him inside the station. He had bit the rope in two, simply because he could and felt he needed to make some kind of protest, but he understood that this stay meant stay and he hadn't left the building.

He hadn't liked it, though, and he hadn't liked the fact that they remained close to home for the next couple of days. Even after that, they had not hunted, which frustrated him. He wanted to hunt. That was what made him what he was.

"Look," Achille said and pointed. "An aardvark."

Thor had scented the creature some time before, but as it ambled into sight ahead, his ears perked, and he stood on his hind legs to get a better look. It smelled like a not-Zoo animal, as did all those here, but it looked like a Zoo animal. He bounded ahead a few feet to see it more clearly. The animal noticed him and began to dig furiously.

"There he goes," the ranger said with a laugh. "The master digger. That's how they protect themselves from their enemies."

Within a minute, the aardvark was halfway underground while dirt scattered between its legs. Thor ran up to it, curious. The creature spun onto its back with the hole protecting it and four feet poised to lash out.

"Come, Thor!" Achille shouted. "You don't want him to kick."

He nosed forward and the aardvark struck and a clawed foot missed his nose by inches. Only his superb reflexes saved him from a nasty scratch.

"Let's go. Leave him alone, Thor."

The ranger took his horns and pulled him away. Thor let him but he constantly turned to watch and within moments, the aardvark had dug enough of the dirt to be completely out of sight.

They made a wide loop and had begun to head home when the breeze brought him another scent—human, and probably food. Thor didn't know how he identified between friend-human and food-human, but he was sure about it.

"What is it, Thor? You sense something?"

He looked at Achille, woofed quietly, then trotted ahead slowly and zig-zagged a little as he triangulated. The food had stopped a little ahead but had continued from there. Something smelled off, though, and Thor stopped to investigate. He nosed into a tiny animal trail and something closed around his nose with a thwang.

Startled, he pulled back in surprise and whatever had caught him slipped free to dangle above the low bushes.

"A snare," Achille said and stepped forward to yank the wire down. "Not that it's strong enough to catch you, Thor." He was quiet for a moment before he added, "It could have snared a paw, though, and it would have been hard to get off."

He cut it free from the tree before he folded it and put it in his pack.

"So, that's what you smelled. A poacher. He's been here recently," he added as he dropped to his knees to finger a footprint in the dirt.

Thor now knew that poacher was another sound for food-human. Achille stood and he lowered his head and slid his right horn under the man's hand. When his friend closed his fingers, he began to lead him in the direction of the food-human.

"You want to get him, right?" Achille asked when he stopped.

He responded with a soft whine.

"I don't know," Achille said.

Which, of course, Thor didn't understand, but he could sense the hesitation in his friend's tone.

The ranger looked in the direction Thor attempted to lead him in and back in the direction of the station. He took another step, stopped, and looked at the human again.

"Okay, okay. Let's see what we have. It's not our fault if they're breaking the law here."

Once Achille was moving, Thor nosed the ground and followed the trail. Twice more, they found snares, which Achille dismantled. But they were getting close and the animal settled onto his belly and wriggled forward while his friend crawled behind him.

There, five bounds ahead, a food-human removed something from a snare. The animal had been dead for a while, its body stiff. The barefoot and raggedly-clothed food-human whistled as he freed the snare from the corpse's neck.

"A jackal," Achille muttered to himself.

Thor brought his hind legs beneath him, ready to spring forward at Achille's, "Kill!"

"You shouldn't be poaching in the park, my brother," Achille muttered. "This is on your own head, not mine. You brought this on yourself.

"Thor, ki—" he started before he suddenly grasped his tail as he launched himself forward.

The ranger held on tightly enough to yank him off balance.

"No. Come!" he hissed.

Thor was confused, but he knew come. He glanced at

the food-human, who still whistled as he held the animal up to admire it without realizing that he was mere meters away from a violent death.

"I know you want to get him, Thor, but you saw him," Achille said after he pulled Thor back and out of sight. "He isn't like the others. This is just some dirt-poor villager trying to feed his family. He can't sell jackal bush meat. No one would buy it. No, this is for him or his family to eat themselves. Against the law, but not worth the death penalty."

With a firm grasp on his right horn, the ranger led him away.

CHAPTER SIXTEEN

Achille

The lorry blew its horn as it bowled past Achille, who pedaled his bicycle while Thor loped alongside. The ranger almost rode into the ditch.

Keep your head on straight!

If the driver noticed anything different about Thor, he didn't intend to stop, but they couldn't risk having the dog seen. Other vehicles had passed earlier but he had made sure to leave the road before the drivers could see that Thor was anything different than a normal dog. This time, he'd been lost in his thoughts and somehow missed the lorry that had sped past.

Achille had been deep into his thoughts far more than usual lately. His quixotic quest to use Thor to rid the park of poachers had not played out as he'd expected. The incident with the local poacher had bothered him more than he wanted to admit. Yes, he'd stopped Thor in time, but barely.

Who was he, Achille Amadou, to pass judgement on

others? To decide if they should live or die? He had not been a devout Christian since his wife and child had died, but still, "Thou shalt not kill," was a good start on living a moral life.

He could justify the five mercenary poachers. They'd tried to kill him and that was obvious self-defense. But hunting others began to attack the walls of justification he'd erected in his mind.

Who was the one with the Mauser? Did he have a family who still waited for him to come home? Could he have stopped the man short of killing him?

For the last week, he had refused to stray far from the station. He was afraid he'd find sign of poachers and equally afraid he'd have to take action. It was better to not know.

He had no choice now, however. A call had come in to report a dead body at a well-known spring. Loko had told him to investigate it, so once again, he was on his bicycle heading north along the RNIE7.

Achille hoped he wouldn't find anything there, and even if someone had died, there would be a good chance that the body was gone, a victim of the scavengers in the area. He'd report back, and that would be the end of it. They didn't have the resources to search the park for a body that might or might never have been real.

They reached the track he needed, and he pulled off the road, his balloon tires softening the jolts of the trail. He really should walk the bicycle to avert a flat tire, but he wanted to get in and out as quickly as possible.

Tall trees ahead signaled that he approached the spring.

"Ho! I am coming," he sang to give fair warning to any

animals that might have gathered there for a drink. He didn't want to surprise anything to the point where they lashed out.

Generations of men had used the spring and pounded a good section of dirt on the east side hard and flat as an access point to the water. Achille and Thor approached from the southwest, so they had to circle to reach the access point. He dismounted from his bicycle and pushed it a little farther before he stopped in his tracks.

There was a body, after all. Not in the spring itself but hung naked by its feet so its arms stretched toward the ground beneath.

He crossed himself when his childhood masses took over momentarily.

Dried blood, brown against the dark skin, covered most of the corpse. No one hung a body like that as an act of kindness, but it was obvious that the poor man had been ill-used.

Thor sat, looked at the body, and whined.

"I know, I know, Thor. It's terrible."

This was a crime scene, and it shouldn't be disturbed. But this was Benin, not Miami, USA. Beninese CSI couldn't look at a scene and magically determine the guilty party. If they could even get a CSI team out to the bush. It was a long way and someone killed in the forest would not be a high priority.

The man deserved proper care. Achille thought he could cut him down, wrap him in the sheet of plastic he'd put into his pack before heading out, and flag down the next truck to transport it back to the station.

"Stay," he ordered Thor before he approached it.

He didn't need the dog's huge footprints on the scene.

The closer he got, the more damage to the back, buttocks, and legs he could see. It looked to him as if the poor man had been beaten to death. He must have gone through agony.

Achille took the man's blood encrusted hand tentatively and spun him slowly. He immediately gasped when he recognized who it was.

The eyeless face of Ranger Josaphat Yassou—the man who'd taken over the investigation into the mercenary camp—stared at him from empty sockets.

"You take care of him, okay?" Achille told Antoine, one of the staff rangers at the Tanguieta station at Pendjari.

"Don't worry. I'll take him to his family," the man said. He looked in the back where Josaphat's wrapped body lay and added, "Bad way to go, Achille. Real bad."

That's an understatement if I've ever heard one.

Poor Josaphat had a multitude of broken bones and a score of cuts over his body. They'd never know how many as there'd be no autopsy for him. He'd been dead for more than a day, and Antoine would deliver the body to his family so he could be prepared for burial.

Achille burned, his rage dampened to red hot coals during the time and effort he'd put in to move the body to his small station. It had been a struggle to carry it, supported by his bicycle seat and handlebars, to the highway. Once there, he'd left Thor in the trees, flagged down a pickup driver, and forced him at gunpoint to take Josaphat and him back to the station. The driver had been terrified, and part of the ranger was sorry for that, but anger clouded his actions. The man had almost jumped out of his skin when he'd yelled "Home!" out of the window as they started off.

Thor understood and arrived only thirty minutes after the terrified driver left his unwelcome passengers and hurried away.

Now, as Antoine drove off, the dampened coals of rage began to fan up again. Josaphat had been killed—almost assuredly by the mercenary poachers—as a warning to the authorities. They were to be left alone by the rangers to do whatever it was what they were doing. And Achille knew it wasn't only poaching. They might take the ivory, they might harvest timber, but those were merely means to an end, a way to pay the bills. These people, whoever they were, had a different end-game planned, one that was not in the interest of the Benin, Burkina Faso, and Niger region.

Achille was only one man, albeit one man with a deadly…dog. But maybe there were others he could count on.

He'd been about to pull back from his war on poachers —or his quasi-legal war, at least. Now, he was determined to keep it going. Not against the local villagers, though—he'd arrest those—but against people like the animals who'd killed Josaphat. They didn't deserve the protection of the legal system.

As he thought of his fellow ranger, he had to take a seat. The young man, so much like him, had taken over after he had been shot. In his heart, he knew that was what killed him. The mercenaries had found the ranger who was tracking them and punished him in their violent—and permanent—way.

Josaphat was killed because of him, Achille Amadou.

Overcome with emotion, he collapsed on the steps to the station, his face down on his arms as sobs wracked him. A moment later, Thor crept up quietly, licked his hand, and forced his head into his friend's lap.

His rough fur soaked up the tears as they fell on him.

CHAPTER SEVENTEEN

Thor

Scents bombarded him, almost too intense to bear, but Thor continued to sit with his nose out the window. He couldn't help himself. It was addictive.

After the friend-human had been killed, Achille had alternated between anger and despair but with a sense of purpose beneath it. They hadn't left for the bush, but the human was busy doing things beyond Thor's ken.

Two days later, he tied him inside the station and disappeared but returned before dusk with a car. Thor knew nothing about cars, but even he could tell that this one was barely functional.

Then came the fake ruff. As Thor grew, his ruff became fuller and gave his throat a degree of protection. The night when he returned with the car, Achille had attached another ruff, this one made from grasses sewn together.

He didn't like it and shook it off. The man replaced it. He shook it off again.

"No, Thor! Leave it on," Achille said finally. "I need to disguise you."

He attached it one more time, and when he started to shake his head, he caught his snout and held him fast.

"You need to keep it on, Thor," he said.

Achille led him to the cracked mirror near his bed and stood him in front of it. "See, you look like a lion. Or, at least, like a dog disguised as a lion like those rich ladies do with their little dogs."

Thor understood lion, and somehow, it clicked. Achille wanted him to look like a lion. Not that he did. He looked nothing like one, but with his horns hidden from sight, it might work from a distance.

"There, now you can come with me tomorrow."

Thor was happy to get it off and less happy when Achille put it back on the next morning. He was even less happy when he pushed him into the car.

It reminded him that he had ridden in a car before when Charles had brought him to Achille. This was nothing like that. When the ranger started it, a blast of black smoke belched out the back and made its way slowly inside. He coughed and was ready to jump out, but it was already moving.

Several sticks were thrown at it as the car crept down the path, and Thor threw up. Achille didn't take notice, his eyes fixed ahead in intense concentration.

They reached the highway and things improved immediately. The smell of smoke disappeared, and with his nose out the window, the glorious assault on his nostrils commenced. He couldn't get enough of it. Most of the smells were familiar except far more saturated as if they pounded into his nostrils. Others were new to him, and he wondered what they were. He stared out the window and tried to identify them, but the car moved too fast for him to really see anything.

Several times, they reached areas teeming with humans. Achille pulled him in and closed the window. The man watched carefully as they made their way slowly through these areas. People saw him and most pointed and laughed.

"C'est drole. Un chien habillé en lion," one man told Achille and held up a little female human to see. The human cub stared at Thor with wide eyes and had one of her fingers in her mouth.

There was too much for him to absorb in these areas, and with the windows up, it was hot and the smell of smoke crept back inside. But beyond the human areas, with the window open, he was elevated to another existence. He never would have imagined that simply sitting in a car with his nose out the window could be so exciting.

It was late afternoon when they made their way through a large area with more humans than Thor had ever seen. He'd never thought about it but in retrospect, he'd never imagined there were so many. There were more there than all the animals in the Zoo combined.

He became antsy. His fake ruff itched and Achille seemed tense, which had an effect on him. Finally, the car came to a stop. The ranger took a few moments to gather himself before he slid out of the car and moved around to open his door.

Thor was happy to get out and he looked for a place to do his thing, but Achille fumbled behind the fake ruff to grab a horn and pulled him forward. They approached a small, square building, barely the size of one of the sheds at the station. Achille, one hand still on Thor's horn, knocked on the door, which opened a few moments later to reveal an older man.

"Achille Amadou, *Nɛ̌a ɖè gbɔn?*" the man asked and his face broke into a brilliant smile.

Instead of replying immediately, Achille removed the fake ruff from Thor.

"Godwin Ogouyemi, I want you to meet Thor," he told the shocked man.

CHAPTER EIGHTEEN

Achille

"I think he is an orisha, sent by Aja. Like her, but just a lesser one," Godwin said as Thor lay at Achille's feet. "There is no other explanation. Not now."

Achille sighed. He wouldn't fight his friend. If that was what he wanted to believe, so be it. It was more than he could have hoped for that he'd taken Thor's mere existence so readily.

Godwin Ogouyemi was a Fon, the largest tribal group in Benin. They held most of the positions of power in the country, and Godwin had been born to comfortably affluent parents, the oldest of five children.

But something had gone wrong with the carefully laid plans of his parents. Instead of taking over the family business, finding a wife, and creating grandbabies, Godwin had jumped from one cause to the other and steadfastly decried all he judged as wrong with society.

He'd spent time as a ranger and vowed to save the environment, and this was how Achille had met him. The man had lasted only a few years before he felt the position was stifling, more routine than revolutionary. But the two had remained close.

His biggest sin, from his family's point of view, however, was when he began to champion LGBTQ rights. He didn't know if his friend was gay and he didn't care if he was or not, but even a hint of that was enough for many, if not most, Benin families to cut ties with the suspected family member.

And that was why he lived as he did in a dark, waterless shack while his family lived in nice houses in the better parts of the city. It was also why Achille was there, even if he felt ashamed of his reasons. Godwin had no one and he was addicted to causes. The ranger needed help and he decided this was his best chance to get it.

So, he if wanted to believe that Thor was Aja or one of her minions and if that would convince him to help, he was willing to exploit that. Godwin was a friend but the cause was bigger than that.

"So, what do you say? Are you willing to put the uniform on again? To help me with this scourge?"

Godwin looked over folded hands and stared at him for a long moment before he asked, "And how can you do this? You are just a field ranger. Has Loko approved it?"

Not exactly, but that doesn't matter.

And it didn't. One of the legacies of the BOHICA Warriors' largess was that Achille controlled the purse-strings of their endowment. The details were murky, worked out between Booker and the president himself, but the bottom line was that the Warriors had exclusive managerial rights over a huge chunk of the park as outside contractors. All the ranger knew was that they provided funds to assist in the upkeep, and all he had to do was contact them if he needed anything.

Even Loko didn't know the extent of their support as most of it was off the books. As far as he was concerned, they were simply another NGO but one with friends in high places. If they "requested" that Godwin get his old job back, Loko wouldn't give it a second thought.

"It is already done, my friend," he said. "Just waiting for you to agree."

"And I have to speak English?" he asked.

For an educated man, Godwin's English was heavily accented, almost to unintelligibility. He spoke better French than Achille, and he spoke Fon and Yoruba, of course. But Thor had been taught commands in English, and he did not intend to try to shift him to one of the other languages.

"Certain words, yes. For him," he said and patted Thor's head.

His friend leaned back and he could see his mind racing as he considered the possibilities.

There was one other characteristic about Godwin that Achille counted on. His friend had a streak of mean in him. He'd knocked heads with police often enough during protests and sometimes went out of his way to confront them. A big man, he was still a force to be reckoned with even as he approached sixty.

"It is a shame about what they did to the Yassou boy. I knew his father."

"Yes, it was."

Time to set the hook.

"They broke every bone in his body while he was still alive. They tortured that fine young man."

Godwin's eyes flared and reminded Achille how Thor's eyes flared red when he was excited.

"Your orisha, there, is proof that this is righteous. If you'll have me, I'm with you."

CHAPTER NINETEEN

Thor

They were on the hunt again. There was no mistaking it. Achille and this new Godwin-human were in full hunt mode, and that excited Thor. It had been too long. He might eat the food Achille brought him each morning, but he was still a creature of the Zoo, part of a hunting pack, and hunting packs…well, hunted.

His might consist of only the two humans and him, but it was his pack with Achille as the alpha.

The two humans stopped and crouched to examine the spoor on the trail.

"*Marun wa—*" Godwin started before Achille interrupted him with, "English."

Godwin rolled his eyes and gave Thor a quick glance before he said, "There are five of them. Too many for us."

Thor had become better and better at understanding Achille. He still couldn't replicate the sounds the humans made but almost as if with the pack, it seemed that the ranger and he were bonding on another level.

Not so with Godwin. He never understood what the human tried to tell him.

"Let's just follow and see what happens."

Both men crept along the trail, their weapons at the ready. Thor walked alongside, unconcerned. He knew there were no food-humans near.

A yip of a hyena reached them, and he perked his ears. He didn't consider the hyenas food, but he was somewhat wary of them after the fight to save the young human. Achille ignored the sound, but Godwin jerked his head up and pointed his rifle in that general direction.

The hyena kept its distance, and they continued deeper into the bush until Achille pointed to the ground and said, "See, those two tracks are going off this way. That's heading to the area where the villager said he'd been taken."

"They kidnapped a villager to help cut down mahogany? And then they let him go?" Godwin asked.

"It happens," Achille explained. "They need labor sometimes."

"Okay. Let's follow them. Better odds, two against two and an orisha."

They followed the trail and Thor heard the chopping long before he could scent the food-humans. Before long, the humans heard it too and slowed to a stop.

"Down by the river, I think. Makes sense. They can float the logs out," Achille said.

Thor padded a rhythm impatiently with his front paws, anxious to get on with the hunt, but the two humans waited, their heads together as they made their noises to each other. Finally, they started out again. He took the lead, all his senses attuned to what was in front of them.

They spooked a small herd of hartbeast, but he didn't give them a second glance. He wanted food-humans.

"Thor, stop," Achille said and pulled his tail as the prey's scent reached him. There were more than two ahead. Probably five, Thor decided, his nose in the air.

"Stay here."

That dreaded word, stay.

He whined in frustration but obeyed and sat on the trail with Godwin while the other man crept forward. Thor listened and tracked Achille as the man approached the much louder group of food-humans.

His friend went silent, and Thor stood, trembling with his instinct to move forward, but the word had power. Godwin put his hand on his back and he accepted it.

After too long, Achille started on his way back. Thor bounced up and down on his front paws in eagerness. The man had been hurt before by the food-human's rifles and he wouldn't calm until he was back there with him.

At last, Achille crept out of the bush. "There's more than two. I counted four mercenaries and a villager. I don't think the villager is there voluntarily. He's the one cutting the tree. Mahogany. They've already cut two, ready to be stripped and shoved into the river."

"Five? That's more than we thought."

"Four poachers. One villager. And they don't seem to be too concerned about getting caught. Only one has his rifle with him, and that's slung on his back. The others have them on an ATV."

Godwin patted the rifle Achille had given him and said,

"We can cut them down before they have a chance to get their weapons."

"We have to give them a chance to surrender," he said.

"Surrender? Why the hell would we do that? They're mercenaries. You know what they did to the Yassou boy."

"No, I don't. I don't know if these are the same ones. All I know is that they're illegally logging."

"You're too soft, Achille my friend. You're going to need to be more cutthroat when the revolution comes. So, we're just going to let them have a chance?"

"A chance to surrender."

"Well, we'd better be ready to run, old man, if they get to their weapons. Four against two, in case you forgot."

"And Thor."

He perked up at his name.

"And what will he do?"

"He's going with us. If they decide to fight, Thor can circle and attack them from the side."

Godwin laughed but kept it low, then asked, "And how are you going to do that? Just tell him?"

"Yes. Oh, I know, it sounds weird, but lately, it's like we understand each other. Sometimes, I'm sure I know what he's thinking."

"Yeah, and Boko Haram will give up their ways, too—hey, do you think these are Boko Haram?" he asked and concern tinged his voice.

"No. They're too uniform, like they have big money behind them."

"And they're bothering with three trees?"

Achille shrugged, then knelt beside Thor with one arm around his neck as he stared into his eyes.

"Thor, we are going forward. I will talk to the enemy. If the enemy fire their rifles, kill. No rifle, no kill."

He cocked his head and whined. While he understood he was to kill the food-humans with rifles, he knew there was more to it than that.

"Yes, I see he understands everything," Godwin said sarcastically.

"Enemy, uniform, rifle, kill. No uniform, no kill."

Thor couldn't understand all the words, but it began to sink in. Kill the food-humans with the rifle but don't kill if they don't have the rifle. He wasn't sure how he knew this, but it wasn't totally new to him. This was much in the same way the pack communicated with each other. Certain sounds meant certain things, but the details were simply understood.

He turned to attack when Achille caught his tail to stop him.

"Not now, Thor. Wait until I say so."

"I have to trust in the orisha," Godwin said. "He's not just a dog."

The three picked their way forward and remained as quiet as they could. The sounds of chopping halted and the three froze until it resumed again.

They reached the heavier vegetation along the river without incident. Achille kept a firm grasp on Thor's horn as they inched forward, the two humans crouched low.

A tree shuddered with a sharp crack and the top of it tilted a little ahead of them but didn't fall. Voices cried out, then the chopping started again and each blow made the top of the tree shake.

After two more steps, the scene unfolded before them.

A food-human chopped the tree. Four other food-humans watched while they talked between themselves.

Achille pointed to Godwin, who moved over a few meters and slithered onto his belly. He peered ahead and gave his teammate a thumbs-up.

After a deep, slow breath, Achille stepped around the tree in front of them and shouted, *"Arrêt. Je suis le garde forestier Amadou. Vous êtes en état d'arrestation,"* followed immediately by *"Idapada. Emi ni Ranger Amadou. O wa labẹ imuni."*

The reaction was immediate. The human chopping the tree dropped his axe and turned, his hands high in the air. The other four didn't hesitate. Three lurched for their rifles while the other unslung his.

"Kill!" Achille shouted and swept one arm in what Thor realized was his friend telling him to attack from around and not head on, exactly as he'd done as a member of the pack. The two rangers opened fire while he bolted to the side and raced down the hill to the river.

One, then another of the food-humans fired. Thor knew they could shoot him and he understood that it could be lethal, but there was no fear as he closed the distance. He reached the river and pivoted to head directly toward them. The first one was on his knees, his rifle to his shoulder as he fired. He didn't see Thor, who lowered his head and rammed his horns into the human's neck.

With a quick twist, he freed his head and barely slowed before he surged at a second two-leg. This one saw him and swung his weapon around, but too late. He caught one arm in his jaws and crunched hard to break bone. The man screamed and fell to his knees, which brought his throat to his attacker's level. It was too easy. All he needed to do was clench his jaw and pull hard, and most of the neck came with it. Blood sprayed and the food fell face-first and scrabbled weakly at the dirt for a couple of seconds before he went still.

The blood lust flowed, and Thor looked for another target. Two of the others were down. One was still with half his head gone. One clutched his belly and a growing red patch stained his shirt. He pointed at Thor and mouthed something silently, his eyes wide as the animal approached.

Instead of biting the food-human, he ducked his head and brought it up quickly again. His right horn caught the man under his chin and stuck. Thor couldn't shake the body loose and had to lean down, put a paw on it, and pull himself free.

Blood dripped in front of his eyes as he looked for another target. The human who'd chopped the tree looked at him with abject fear. Urine ran down his leg.

Thor intended to savor this. His head held low, he uttered a low growl as he stalked the cowering human.

"No, Thor! Friend!" Achille screamed and raced forward.

It took a moment for that to register. Thor stood rigidly and looked around. The ranger ran to him and waved his arm.

"No, no! He's a friend!"

He looked from Achille to the other human and back again before his killing lust began to fade.

His friend had said, "No rifle, no kill." This human had

something with which he attacked the tree, but it wasn't a rifle.

He stopped, sat, and waited for Achille. The human rolled his eyes and collapsed onto the dirt.

"Good boy, good boy," Achille said and patted him on the shoulders.

Behind him, Godwin approached slowly. When he reached them, he went down on one knee, and said, "All respect, orisha."

CHAPTER TWENTY

Achille

Something didn't sit right with him, but he couldn't put his finger on it. Achille stared into the forest and tried to apply himself to finding the source of his discomfort.

Their last mission had been a resounding success. He'd given the poachers a chance to surrender and they'd chosen to fight. He and Godwin had managed to eliminate two of them—Godwin claimed both, something he wouldn't argue. Thor had dealt with the other two and finished off one of those they'd shot.

The dog had been masterful and he'd somehow understood that he wanted him to attack the poachers from the flank. It had worked perfectly. More impressive, however, was that he had let Achille call him off the villager. He had feared for the worst when he was in his killing mode, but in one second, he was a demon and in the next, a lovable pet dog.

He smiled when he thought of the villager. The man had passed out. He wondered what he would think when he woke up with four dead bodies, and would he even tell those back in his village? Achille doubted it.

The smile faded as he returned to the mission at hand. It was too soon for them to be out again, but Godwin had insisted. He'd been so psyched about the poachers that he wanted more. That night in the station, he'd cleaned the Uzi Achille had bought for him and relived each moment over and over again. He wanted more, and against his better judgement, his friend had given in.

They might not even find sign of anyone today. They were a little far from where most of the activity had been, heading toward the river where Thor had first met the elephants. He hadn't been able to stand against Godwin's insistence, but at least he'd steered them to where contact was unlikely.

The trail followed a slight decline and passed through mostly grasslands with the occasional tree here and there. Up ahead, it entered a thicker forest before it turned to run along the riverbank. He'd taken tourists there before—the last a group of school kids—and he'd rarely seen signs of illegal activity. It was too much in the open for the poachers.

So why was he uneasy? There were almost no signs of wildlife, but it was barely after noon on a hot day. The animals might merely be holed up trying to keep cool under the shade of trees or down at the river.

"Well," Godwin commented. "We can't catch ourselves terrorists if we don't go looking."

The man had elevated the mercenary poachers to terrorists that morning. He now carried an American

Springfield XDS .45 along with his Uzi—"Ready for anything," he'd said.

Achille looked at Thor to see if he sensed anything. The dog seemed normal, which for him was an eagerness to get on with it.

I guess I'm just being paranoid. Godwin's right. We can't find them if we're too afraid to go on.

"Let's go," he said and strode out of their cover. "Keep your eyes open for sign."

He led the way down the trail but felt naked and exposed. Up ahead, the thicker forest would give them better concealment.

A screeching secretary bird erupted from the grass and almost gave him a heart attack as it fought to gain altitude. He laughed and looked at Godwin when a distant chatter of gunfire reached him. Before he could turn in that direction, the ground around him dissolved into chaos as pieces of vegetation shrapneled around them and the buzz of hornets zipped past.

"Get down!" he shouted but his friend's head and shoulders disappeared in a mist of pink. Godwin's body fell with a thud.

"Godwin!" he shouted as he scrambled on his hands and knees to reach him.

He knew there was nothing he could do but instinct took over. The staccato burst of another barrage of automatic fire reached him, and he flung himself as low as he could while heavy rounds impacted around him.

"Thor!" he shouted and looked around wildly.

There was a yelp and Thor tumbled.

Achille looked at Godwin. His body didn't even twitch

and there was no sign of his head. He shifted and scrambled to Thor.

The dog tried to regain his feet. The top half of his right horn was shattered and he seemed dazed. He reached him and traced his hands over his body. The animal didn't seem wounded aside from his horn.

In the distance, the sound of a diesel engine reached him. Achille had to see and darted up. Some kind of armored vehicle in the distance, maybe six hundred meters away on a piece of high ground, now headed their way.

Stupid!

In this mix of grassland and forest, view was not unlimited in all directions, but it could reach up to a kilometer or even more in corridors. That armored vehicle had probably sat there and simply waited for someone to come into view—specifically, armed rangers. The three of them had almost assuredly been seen earlier, and the mercenaries had bided their time until they had a clear shot. Now, they were coming to finish them off.

Who has armored personnel carriers except for the Army?

Oh, hell. The Army?

Achille couldn't sit and wait for the vehicle to make its way over to them. He had no way to fight it and there was only one thing to do.

Run.

CHAPTER TWENTY-ONE

Thor

On the station's porch, Thor twisted his head and ran his paw along his horns. The broken one was still rough with no sign of regeneration.

He still wasn't sure what had happened. One moment, he was with Achille and Godwin, and the next, he was hit in the horn. Dazed, he'd barely been aware of Achille pulling him to his feet and forcing him to run.

There had been the sounds of something big pursuing them, but the two had managed to reach denser forest and escape.

Godwin wasn't with them.

For two days now, they'd stayed at the station. Thor healed quickly, but he was grateful for the first day. Now, by the second day, he was ready to retaliate. He wasn't sure what had hurt him, but he knew it was the food-humans.

Achille had been agitated, however, and spent time making sounds into his "radio." He'd taken out more of his rifles and left them near every window of the station.

The two of them had been developing a bond between them, one that made understanding easier, but now, he was lost. He had no idea what was going on, and he wanted his life to return to normal.

With the ranger on the radio once again, Thor lay on the porch with his head across his crossed paws, half asleep.

A familiar scent tickled the back of his nose and he whined and rubbed a paw over his snout until it registered fully. As if shocked by the wires on the Zoo's wall, he bolted to his feet and careened down the steps and the path while he howled to the world.

Thor leaped at the large figure and his jaws opened as his feet pounded into his chest and knocked him to the ground.

"Nice to see you too, you big oaf," Charles said as Thor tried to lick him to death.

CHAPTER TWENTY-TWO

Achille

"So, you don't know who these people are?" Charles asked. Thor lay contently at his feet.

Achille shrugged and said, "Not specifically, no. They've got money, which means they have very important people in back of them."

"I don't get it, though. All this effort for elephant ivory and mahogany? Is all of that worth killing for?"

"I don't think that's the raison d' être. It may be a way to keep the mercenaries sharp while paying the bills."

"And you're sure they are mercenaries? I mean, those guys fight wars."

"And what is this but a war against the park?" the ranger snapped a little more forcibly than he'd intended.

Achille was in a foul mood. He blamed himself for Godwin's death. That was two—him and Josaphat. If he'd simply kept his head down and eyes averted, both men would still be alive. But for all Godwin had carried on about Thor being an orisha, how was he any different?

He'd been presented with this magical creature and given resources, and somehow, his ego was so big that he thought he could take on the mercenaries?

Be realistic, Achille. You're an old man, not Superman.

"Sorry," he said. "I'm calling them mercenaries. They could be commercial poachers, backed by a big corporation. They could be a militia or a rebel group. Or they could be something bigger."

"Like the Army? What kind of APC did they have?" Charles asked.

"I don't know. It had a big machine gun."

"Did you see markings on it?"

"I was more interested in running."

The American rubbed the stub of Thor's horn absent-mindedly and said, "If it was the Army, then we've got problems."

"We?"

"If it's militia or a terrorist group, that's still bad," he said, talking more to himself than to his companion. "Do you think it could be Oladipupo? He's the one who arranged for the kidnapping of the schoolgirls and Sophie."

Achille shrugged again. He had no idea who it could be.

A large part of him wished the big American would take Thor and disappear from his life. He would never have gone down this path if the BOHICA Warriors had not shown up to save those schoolgirls, and he should have refused when they'd returned and asked him to take care of Thor.

When he'd explained what had happened, Charles hadn't seemed surprised and he'd admitted that Thor had killed a man before. That had made him angry. He should not have been kept in the dark.

But when he looked at Thor where he lay on top of the man's feet, he felt a pang of jealousy. He'd grown attached to the dog and they'd built up an unspoken bond.

"It seems to me that these guys are playing for keeps, whoever they are. And that might mean you're in danger," Charles said.

Achille shrugged yet a third time.

"Let me ask you this. I can get you out of here. Maybe up to the Zoo. Roo is running things there for us now. Maybe to the US. You'd be safe, at least. Or, if you had the chance, what do you want to do about these guys—the ones who killed your friends?"

Pent up anger broke through the mental dam he'd erected, and there was only one possible answer. "I want to kill them," he all but snarled.

The big man nodded and said, "I need to leave you two here while I go arrange things. I guess it's good to have friends in high places."

CHAPTER TWENTY-THREE

Thor

Charles had come back but now, he was gone again and Thor was depressed because he didn't know why. Achille was still around, but that wasn't the same. He cared for the ranger, but he wasn't Charles.

He waited each day at the end of the path. While he could still detect the faintest scent of his friend there, that was all. It was as if his return had been a dream.

Mr. Ogbé seemed happy to have him back in his sights, but after an initial flurry of sticks without a reaction from him, the little two-leg seemed to tire and now sat on a low-hanging branch and watched him.

His presence made Thor feel a little better. Not much, but a little.

Achille's tension also weighed on him. He still had that connection, and he felt the man's nervousness. While he waited for Charles, his nerves were alive and his senses on high alert. Every snap of a twig, every distant shout, and every vehicle on the main highway brought him to his feet.

He wanted to run and blow off energy but worried that he might miss Charles coming back, so he watched from his chosen position and simply waited.

One of the human vehicles drove past, then stopped. Thor sat, his ears attuned. Trees blocked the highway from his view but not the sound. The car began to reverse, and he pushed to his feet as a low growl emanated from the bottom of his throat.

The car stopped again before it drove off the road and onto the path. He sniffed the air but all he could smell was car and fuel, nothing else.

He knew he could slink into the forest. Achille had trained him to do that for when someone was coming to the station, but the past events had him on edge. He didn't want to slink off, waiting for the ranger to call him forward. Achille feared for his life now, and the car coming could be the enemy.

Thor stood in the middle of the path as a blockade. If this was the enemy, they'd have to get through him first. He snarled, pulled his teeth back, and expanded his ruff.

The vehicle came to a stop in front of him. He snarled louder.

The window came down and a voice said, "Is this the way you greet me, Thor?"

He bounded forward and put his front paws on the edge of the open window to lean in and lick Booker's face. While he'd never been as close to this friend-human, anyone was a relief at this stage.

"You sure he remembers you, Booker?" another voice asked.

Thor lowered his head to look at the other human. It

was the female Reen human. He had no relationship with her but he knew she was a friend of Charles, and that was good enough for him.

"So, where's Charles, boy?" Booker asked.

Thor jumped at the name and yipped with joy. He stuck his head in the car but he knew immediately the big man was not there. There was no Charles smell.

"Calm down, Thor. We're obviously in the right spot, so let's go see."

The car started to move slowly, and he dropped to the ground. He trotted alongside as they made their way up the path. Mr. Ogbé stared at him with black eyes, but he didn't throw anything.

Achille was at the window and the muzzle of a rifle protruded. Thor barked and wished he could say friend in human sound. Instead, he tried to imagine Booker and projected friend. The muzzle wavered, but it did not withdraw.

The car came to a stop in front of the station, and the occupants stepped out and stretched to ease the kinks of long hours on the road.

The muzzle vanished and a moment later, Achille appeared at the door. "Mr Booker, I'm surprised to see you here. Why did you come?"

"Achille, I'd say good to see you, but I'm not sure it is. Charles called me—"

"And me," Reen said.

"He said you needed help," the other man continued. "So, here we are. Where is he?"

"Mr Charles said he needed to speak to friends in high

places. Those were his words. He said he should be back tomorrow if all goes well."

Booker looked at Reen and she gave the slightest of nods.

"Well, then, how about you inviting us in for tea and letting us know what the bleddy hell is going on?"

CHAPTER TWENTY-FOUR

Achille

"Are you sure about this?" Achille asked the logger.

"Yes. They are coming for you. They know who you are."

"He says our friends are coming for us," he said in English to the others before he turned to the man once more.

He stared at him for a long moment, then asked, "Why are you telling me this? Doesn't this put your own life in danger?"

"Because you saved my life. I'm living on borrowed time. If they weren't going to kill me, the...orisha, it was coming for me before you called it off."

"But you weren't there by choice."

"True, but I was cutting down the trees. Not them." He hesitated before he asked, "It is true? Is she Aja?"

"I don't know," he said, refusing to label Thor.

"Ask if he knows who they are," Charles said in English.

"He wants to know who they are. Do you know?" Achille asked and reverted to Yoruba.

"They do not say, only that things will change soon. I think they come from many nations, though. Not all speak Yoruba. Some are not even African."

"What do they want?"

"I don't know. Maybe a new country, carved out of the Niger River. They want our young ones to join them."

Achille turned back to Charles and said, "He doesn't know. They're not all from here, though, or even Niger or Burkina Faso. He thinks some aren't even African."

He returned his focus to the logger. "Do you know when they'll come for us?"

The man, who hadn't given his name, swept his gaze at the others in the station and said, "Soon. I only heard your name, though. Not these people. I think..." He paused as if he tried to determine how to word what he wanted to say. "I think that if these people will take you to their country, you should go. Aja herself cannot save you."

The ranger scoffed and said, "I thank you for this, friend. Thank you for the warning."

The man looked like he wanted to say something else but instead, he nodded and stepped off the porch and back into the night.

"So, what did he say?" Booker asked.

"What we expected. They are coming for us. Me. He doesn't think they know about you."

"President Okonkuo thinks the money behind them comes from Cotonou and Lagos, and there's at least one former Burkina Faso general involved."

"Fucking great," Reen said. "We've got ourselves an international coalition."

"And the president can't send in the troops?" the Brit asked.

"No, not yet. None of this is official and he doesn't yet understand the power dynamics. He's trying to form an alliance to make a move but that's not ready yet, and it won't be for a while."

"I bet it's Sophie's father," she said.

"She's still got some contacts down here," Booker said. "Her father might be in a cash-poor situation right now."

"All the more reason to make a move," Charles pointed out.

"At least the president gave us some nice toys." Booker looked over to where enough weapons to outfit an infantry company were stacked. "It would have been nice if he could have given us some trigger-pullers to use them."

"Gentlemen," Achille said before he added hastily, "and lady. I appreciate you coming, but this isn't your fight. Mr Booker, your wife is pregnant and that baby will need a father. Mr Charles and Miss Reen, you are American. This does not concern you. The logger said that these men are coming for me, not you. You can still leave."

"You forgot that we are the managers for this part of the park, Achille. Do you want us to forget about that?"

"No—yes! You don't have to die for this."

Charles gave a wry laugh and said, "Lucky for you, you don't have much to say about that. We're the managers, so I think we need to manage the situation. Right, guys?"

Booker and Reen nodded.

"But there is the fact that there are four of us—four and Thor," Booker said.

Thor's tail thumped on the floor when he heard his name.

"We've got the weapons. Achille, do you think you can get some locals to help?"

Achille had already thought about it. Some of the rangers he knew and trusted, maybe. The villagers? The poor people scrabbled in the dust for a living, pushed one way and another between the government, the militias, and the criminals, and simply tried to stay out of the way. He could try, but he wasn't sure what would happen.

"Some, Mr Booker. I don't know how many will come."

"Well, we do have an advantage. They think that it's only Achille here. I think that makes them the perfect target of an ambush. Hit them hard, bloody their noses, and maybe they'll step back until the president's ready to take action."

"So you will stay and fight?" Achille asked.

"Bleddy hell yeah, we're staying," Booker said before he cleared the table to give him someplace to work. "This is what I'm thinking now…"

CHAPTER TWENTY-FIVE

Thor

He was on another hunt with Achille but this time, Charles was there with him as well. Thor was happy and didn't question things too much.

It had been confusing at first, though. There was the air of the hunt and he could sense that Achille was ready, but they didn't leave. The humans did human things near the station. Mr Ogbé chittered and scolded them from the treetops and showered them with sticks and leaves until he finally gave up and scampered off to join the rest of his troop.

Thor stayed close to Charles, and when his friend placed a small green box against the base of a tree, he moved closer to sniff it.

"Don't get too close, Thor," the man said with a laugh. "Mr Claymore can take your nose right off."

It smelled of metal and nastiness, and he backed away. He was lost as to what the humans were doing. The food-humans were out in the bush, not at the station. Frustrated, he laid down alongside the path and went to sleep while the often-incomprehensible humans did their thing.

Finally, it seemed as if they were ready. They checked their rifles but they didn't leave and chose positions on the ground instead. He stood in the middle of the path and whined in an attempt to will them to move out.

"Not now, Thor," Achille said. "We're doing this right here. Stay!"

The dreaded word. With one more look into the bush, he trotted over to Charles and laid down beside him.

Every little noise caught his attention but the waiting grew too long, and when Charles scratched him gently behind the ears, he drifted off to sleep again.

A sound of a car woke him. He wasn't sure why. Cars occasionally moved along the highway off in the distance, but this was different. It took a moment before he realized what it was. This car was coming to them. It was making its way down the path to the station.

Thor whined and stood, his gaze locked down the path.

"You got something, Thor?" Charles asked.

He responded with a soft yip.

"I think we might have something," the man whispered to the others. "Get ready."

He pulled Thor down and although he wanted to fight it, he acquiesced but his body remained tense and ready to spring forward into the kill.

The car came closer and forged ahead slowly.

"I hear it," Reen said. "Get ready, Booker."

"We need to make sure it's them," he replied.

Thor wiggled his butt, ready to spring into action.

The car drove into view ahead. He could see six food-humans inside, all on the alert. They were on their own hunt as well.

"It's them," Achille said before he turned to him and whispered, "Enemy."

He almost yipped with happiness at the word, but he was a better hunter than that. Instead, he froze, not moving a muscle, and waited for the word—kill.

The car continued its advance, and he waited for the release. Finally, they were abreast of them, only two bounds away.

The blast surprised Thor and startled him. He bolted to his feet, uncertain of what had happened. Unfamiliar smells assaulted his nostrils, along with more familiar smells of blood and death.

The car skidded to a stop, the food-humans inside obviously dead. The car itself was riddled with holes.

"Hooee!" Charles said as he stood, his rifle unfired. "Hello to my little friend, Mr Claymore!"

Reen and Booker stood as well and the two slapped their hands together in excitement before they stepped out into the road.

Another blaring sound grated on Thor's ears and the sound drew closer. At the end of the curve, two food-humans appeared astride what looked to be larger, smellier bicycles and slid to a halt.

"Bleddy hell, there's more of them!" Booker yelled and the four humans opened fire.

Too late, however. The two had turned and retreated around the bend. Thor's instincts kicked in, and despite still being unsettled in the blast, he turned to chase the two.

"Thor, get them!" Charles shouted.

He heard his name, so instead of pursuing the two food-humans, he jumped up on Charles with his front paws on his chest and leaned in to lick his face.

"No, the guys on the motorcycles! Get them!"

He knew the man wanted something but he wasn't sure what. Confused, he dropped down and cocked his head while he tried to understand him.

"Motorcycles!"

"Thor, those two—kill," Achille said and pointed down the path.

Thor didn't need him to point. He understood what he wanted, wheeled about, and raced in a mad dash to pursue the two food-humans, exactly as he'd started to do before Charles had interrupted him.

It felt good to be on the chase and running all out. He'd always been out with Achille and so was limited by his friend's speed, or lack thereof. This was the first time since about forever that he'd been able to extend himself. With a clear running lane, he hurtled down the path and each bound covered huge amounts of ground.

But the food-humans remained ahead of him. The horrible grating noise kept pace, and if he closed the distance at all, it wasn't by much. In another minute, they'd be at the highway.

Thor pushed harder and strained every muscle in his body in attempt to coax more speed. This is where he needed his pack at the Zoo. His kind didn't run prey down —they drove it into a trap and one of them would ambush it. But how could he do that alone and with a prey that was at least as fast as he was?

The noise the two food-humans made became less. He

knew they had reached the big road and a moment later, the noise grew in volume again but came closer to him.

He didn't think it out and simply acted upon instinct. The path intersected the highway at an angle. The food-humans had reached the main route and now returned, and that gave him the chance to ambush them—if he could cut through the bush quickly enough to intercept them.

Thor darted off the path to the right and sprinted through the vegetation. Up ahead and to his left, he caught a glimpse of them through the trees, riding along the highway. If they drew level with him before he could reach the road, he knew he had no chance to catch them.

With a final burst of speed, his lungs heaving, he burst through the final line of forest as the two accelerated past. He broke through the foliage, reached the road, and surged into the attack as the nearest food-human spotted him. His mouth and eyes opened wide an instant before he barreled into him.

The impact knocked Thor off his feet and tumbled him several times across the highway. He scrambled to his feet while the food-human tried to stand and yelled at the other one, who had pulled to a stop a little farther down and looked back. He began to unsling his rifle when Thor, his red eyes blazing, surged toward him.

The food-human took one look, spun, and roared off the other way. Thor gave chase, but one shoulder didn't seem to function as it should and it was clear he'd never catch him. He stopped and watched the food-human disappear down the highway.

Slowly, he turned to the one he'd managed to stop. This man pointed his rifle at him, but Thor could see it was broken and the long part bent. He threw it down, limped to his big bicycle, and tried to right it.

Thor stalked forward, his gaze locked on his prey. The human kicked frantically at it, but the bicycle was dead. He began to shout as the animal approached and screamed sounds he didn't know, but they reeked of fear.

As could be expected when death looked someone in the eyes.

CHAPTER TWENTY-SIX

Achille

He was sixty-five years old now, and while in great shape for his age, time had taken its toll and the three younger people easily outdistanced him. Achille gritted his teeth and struggled to catch up to the others.

The last few minutes had bombarded his emotions. He'd been anxious when the logger had told him he was a target of the still mysterious group of mercenaries. Grateful that he'd not have to face them alone, he'd watched as the other three placed the claymore mines around their "kill zone," as the two US Marines called it. The devices looked small to him and he hadn't really trusted them to do the job. He counted more on each of them and the weapons each had.

The three looked like they were going to war with all they carried—and maybe that was exactly what they were doing. Booker had offered Achille more weapons, but he'd turned him down. He was used to the FN-FAL Mick had given him and didn't want to try to learn something new.

Then, they'd waited. And waited. Thor had been on edge, he could tell. He felt the same way. When the sounds of a technical approached, it had almost been a relief. One way or the other, this would soon be settled.

He was surprised at the anger that blossomed inside him when the Toyota drove into view. Resolute, he flipped the safety off and readied himself mentally as the vehicle, with what looked to be two in the cab and four in the bed, approached the kill zone.

The blast, triggered by Booker, took him by surprise. Four claymores detonated and hundreds of metal balls hurtled—and penetrated—the technical. Achille shouted in exultation as he stood with his weapon ready and looked for a target.

But there wasn't one—or not a living threat, at least. The six men had been riddled. The nearest one in the cab had what was left of his bloody head leaned out the window. The one who'd been on the mounted machine gun in the back had fallen over the edge to lie in a formless heap on the ground. A single arm appeared over the wall of the bed and grasped weakly at nothing before it collapsed inside.

"Hooee!" Charles said as he stood next to Achille. "Hello to my little friend, Mr Claymore!"

He could feel that Thor was confused, but he joined the other three as they checked the Toyota. It was ready for the junkyard, but he was focused on the six occupants. One in the bed was still alive, at least for the next few moments. The others were dead.

With his ears still ringing from the blast, it took him a moment to hear the approaching motorcycles. He looked up as two men appeared at the bend in the road a hundred meters away and skidded their motorcycles to a halt with looks of surprise on their faces.

"Bleddy hell, there's more of them!" Booker yelled.

Achille fired together with the others, but the two had already raced out of sight around the bend.

"Thor, get them!" Charles shouted.

The dog looked at Charles, then jumped up on him, his tail wagging, as he licked the man's face.

"No, the guys on the motorcycles! Get them!"

Achille could sense that Thor was confused. He didn't know what the man wanted.

"Motorcycles!" the American yelled.

Achille had to step in. He knew the danger of letting those two escape.

"Thor, those two, kill," he said and pointed to where the two mercenaries had disappeared.

He could feel the connection and he knew Thor understood. The dog wheeled and surged forward like a rocket in pursuit of the two mercs.

His three team members set off as well, albeit much slower. Achille took one last look at the dead and dying, then followed. The other three outdistanced him, but he continued to run, his ears attuned to the sound of the motorcycles. They were almost out of audible range, but he could hear them slow—they were probably where his drive met the highway—and that meant Thor hadn't caught up to them. A moment later, they revved again and seemed to return.

Of course, they're heading north.

Achille bolted off the path and headed toward the highway. He had to cut them off. Farther down, the drive was closer to the road but here, he probably had about a hundred and fifty meters of bush to break through. He knew he probably wouldn't make it, but he had to try.

In the next moment, he heard the unmistakable sound of a crash. His heart leapt. Thor had caught them! His celebration ended when one bike started again.

His lungs burned and he tried to push himself faster when he caught barely a glimpse of rushing movement through the trees. He fired, but the bush was too dense. The motorcycle continued to drive north.

Achille broke through the bush and looked after it. This was a long, straight stretch of RNIE7 and he could see a single motorcycle maybe five hundred meters away and still going. He fired and emptied his magazine, but the rider continued his flight.

Disheartened, he turned to look south. A motorcycle lay on its side two hundred meters away and the merc tried to right it. Thor—his dog, his pet dog—launched himself at the man. There was no struggle. One moment, the mercenary was standing and in the next, he was down with Thor crouched over him. Achille could hear the crack of bone even as the others appeared at the intersection of his drive and the highway, far beyond Thor and the dead merc. They hadn't known to cut through the bush but had followed the track.

Achille jogged down to Thor and reached him before the others. Blood covered his muzzle and made a fearsome visage that was at odds with the way he looked at him and whomped his tail against the road surface.

He knew that he liked to eat his prey but for some

reason, that shamed him and he didn't want the others to know. He sent a mental plea for him not to eat and to his surprise, Thor sat with his head cocked to the side as he looked at him.

Before he could wonder at that, the others ran up.

"Did you get the other one?" Booker asked.

"No. He was too far away."

"Well, then, it looks like we've got ourselves a problem," he said as he stared down the now-deserted highway.

"What about the other rangers?" Booker asked Achille.

"Some are on their way. I don't know how many."

"We could have used them this morning," Reen said. "They could have cut their avenue of escape off."

He shrugged. These foreigners expected immediate results. Africa didn't work that way. The birthplace of humankind ran to a different beat—a slower, more deliberate beat.

Still, he was glad these foreigners were there. If not, he was sure he'd be dead now, merely one more ranger killed by poachers. He knew that even with Thor, the two of them couldn't have stood up to the assassins.

He glanced at the dog, who lay asleep at Charles' feet. He couldn't help it and once again felt a twinge of jealousy. As if he sensed it, Thor lifted his head off the floor, looked over at him, and gave two weak thumps of his tail before he went to sleep again.

Achille felt in his heart that Thor was apologizing. He was long over being shocked at how he felt he knew what he was thinking and vice versa. But it did fill him with wonderment and curiosity. He didn't know how it was happening. This morning, however, it became clear to him that Thor and Charles didn't have the same rapport and he felt guilty for reveling in that.

"We need to know where and how many they are," the American said. "No word from your buddies?" he asked Booker.

"Not yet."

"However many there are, we need to hit them, and hit them so hard their dicks come out their noses," Reen said.

"That's the Marine I know and love," Booker said. "So ladylike."

She gave him the finger and Achille wondered again at his guests. They obviously loved and respected each other, but it was hard to tell sometimes with the way they criticized and made fun of one another.

"You don't have to know where they are. You can still leave. This is not your fight," he reminded them.

They all rolled their eyes as one as if he'd said the stupidest thing in the world and Booker said, "The key is to take it to them, not let them take the initiative. That's why we need to know how many trigger-pullers we'll have."

Thor suddenly raised his head, pushed to his feet, and ran to the door. The others froze for a moment before Booker nodded to Charles who took Thor by the scruff of the neck and pulled him into the living quarters. The three of them left in the main part of the station picked their weapons up as the sound of a vehicle reached them.

Reen stepped to the side of the window and looked out as the vehicle came to a stop.

"Well, shit," she said as she put her rifle down, walked to the door, and opened it. "Look what the cat brought in."

Mick Bennelong strode into the station, all smiles. Achille smiled equally as widely in response. Of all the BOHICA Warriors he'd met, he felt the closest connection with the Australian Aboriginal. They were creatures cut from the same cloth.

"Sorry I'm late. Didn't get your message until I got back to base."

Reen pounded him on the back, while Booker shook his hand.

"Come on out, Charles. It's Mick," he said as Achille went up to welcome the Australian.

"Glad you could make it," Charles said and gave the shorter man a hug while he lifted him off his feet.

"Put me down you, you bloody Yank!"

"How's Roo?" Reen asked.

"Going cabin-crazy," Mick said. "I almost had to tie him down to keep him from coming with me."

Achille must have looked puzzled because Charles told him, "Roo got in a fight with one of the Zoo critters and he almost lost. He's confined to bed until both legs heal."

He had wondered why the other Australian wasn't there. He didn't particularly care for the acerbic man, but the more people they had, the better chance they had to come through this alive. Besides, Roo excelled in a fight.

"Uh, I've got friends out there waiting to talk to you, Achille," Mick said.

"Friends?"

"I needed a guide to finding this bloody place, and they were it."

Achille walked cautiously to the door and looked out. Five villagers stood there, armed with machetes and homemade spears. One was Fabrice Hounsou, the father of the little girl Thor had saved.

Hounsou stepped forward, gripping the Chinese-made machete that was so new the ever-present rust hadn't stained it yet.

"Bawo ni o se wa, Onija Amadou," he said.

"Bawo ni o se wa, Mister Hounsou," he replied automatically before he asked, "What are you doing here?"

"We are here to help. Reginald here," he said and pointed at one of the others with his machete, "he heard the shooting. He went to investigate and he saw you with the dead man."

Suddenly, Achille wished he'd brought his FN. He glanced back, ready to call for help. He squared his shoulders, faced the man, and made no effort to deny anything.

"And?"

"And we want to help."

He was taken aback. *Help an onija, a ranger?*

"Why?" he managed to ask after a moment.

"Why? Because these devils are bad people. They want our young to fight with them. They've taken girls for jungle wives."

They've taken young? They've got captives?

Achille knew he had to tell this to the others before they made a plan.

"We know you have foreigners here."

"I saw the *yovo,*" Reginald interrupted. "And the other foreign soldiers with you."

Yovo was a term for white person, so they knew Booker

was there along with the others, and that word would spread. They weren't really soldiers but this was neither the time nor place to try to explain things.

"And we know you are good, Onija Amadou. You saved my cousin Daniel from the Orisha."

Achille shook his head in surprise. The logger he'd saved was Hounsou's cousin?

"Daniel is gathering more to help. But when the foreign soldier Mick was lost and asked for help finding you, we came with him. This is our home, and with Aja on our side, we cannot lose."

He looked at the man who returned the stare, full of righteous determination. His machete would not stand up to the mercenaries' weapons, but that was his choice to make. A man made his own choices in life.

"Wait here," he said. "I will tell them."

When he turned to go inside, one of the others asked in a hopeful voice, "Is the Aja here?"

Achille hesitated, looked at the man, then started walking again. He didn't know what to say.

He entered the station to Charles' and Reen's questioning glances, while Booker was on his satphone.

"Some of the local villagers want to help us," he said and didn't go into details.

The Brit spoke quietly on the phone so he remained silent for the next few minutes until the man looked at his iPad and said, "Okay, it's coming in now. Bleddy brilliant. I owe you a pint, Laaek."

He turned to the others and gave them a thumbs-up before he looked at his iPad.

"We've got it?" Charles asked, then added, "I can't

believe it. We're US Marines and we can't do anything, but a Brit SAS can find a buddy back in Merry 'ole England who can call his buddy who knows where to access US Air Force drone images."

"Whatever it takes," Reen said.

"I know, but security must suck big time. I mean, how classified is this?"

Achille followed the conversation but he wasn't quite sure what Charles was saying—not until Booker came over with his iPad and put it on the table. There was a photo of the bush, complete with coordinates. Very clearly, Achille could see the river, which looked like the Pendjari. On one bank was a camp, and he could see individuals.

He had never seen real spy-drone images but he'd watched a few movies that had them. This was a US Air Force image. Why the US Air Force flew over the park was beyond him—and it irked him more than a little—but this was vital information. Why it took Booker, who was British and not Charles or Reen, who had been in the US Marines, was confusing as well.

"Now, we've got a location as of yesterday morning local time, and we can figure out how many there are, courtesy of Uncle Sam's Air Force. Let's figure out what we're going to do."

CHAPTER TWENTY-SEVEN

Charles

"Are you in position, Rambo?" Charles asked over the walkie talkie.

The ranger insisted that was his real name, not a nickname.

"Roger wilco, over and out," Rambo said.

He rolled his eyes. It wasn't proper Marine Corps comms procedures, but Rambo was one of the few rangers who'd joined them who spoke English, and it got the message across.

Having the walkie talkies—in this case, the 50-channel Midland GXT1000s Mick brought down with him—was a huge benefit. The Zoo did not take kindly to radio comms, and Charles had almost forgotten how useful being able to communicate with others was.

Without people trained in comms procedures, Booker had decided to keep the civilians and rangers on two separate frequencies, with Reen talking to the civilians and Charles to the rangers.

He gave the Brit a thumbs-up to let him know that the blocking force of seven rangers was in position. If any of the mercenaries survived the assault and fled back along the river trail, the blocking force was supposed to cut them down.

Now, all they had to worry about was the civilians. Charles had not been in favor of them being part of the assault, but they'd insisted and told them they'd go it alone if they had to. At least this way, they should be out of the actual fighting.

Charles grabbed Thor's front leg and pulled it down. His four-legged friend didn't like the lion mane-like disguise Achille had put on him and constantly pawed at it. He didn't blame him. It looked ridiculous and barely hid his one-and-a-half horns. To him, he looked like a Zoo-creature with a cheap disguise. As few of the other rangers had seen him, however, and they didn't seem to take much notice of him.

He had missed Thor. He'd known he couldn't keep him in the Zoo. Even if word hadn't gotten out that he had killed and eaten Bronson, once people realized he was a Zoo-creature, he'd be killed or taken away to a lab somewhere for study.

Sophie had the idea to bring him to Achille and the W National Park, and Booker had called in a few favors from President Okonkuo. It seemed like a good compromise, but when he returned to the Zoo, Charles had begun to lose interest. Booker and Sophie had left for the UK—not Bristol, where Booker was from, but Edinburgh in Scotland—while they waited for the birth of their baby. Roo gradually took over the day-to-day operations, trained the new hires, and sourced gigs, with Reen and Mick as his lieutenants while the American slowly began to extricate himself from active participation. He'd made considerable money—more than he really needed—and he wanted to see Thor again.

Charles merely never thought he'd come for a visit and find himself in the middle of a war. He'd sent him south to hide him, so he was somewhat surprised—and not too happy—that Achille had used Thor in his vendetta. The demiwolf had even had half his right horn shot off. Zoo-creatures were tough, but he had fought enough of them to know that a round in Thor's head would be all she wrote, and he resented the fact that the ranger had put him into danger. Regardless, he couldn't leave him alone to face his enemies.

He had called his friends as reinforcements, then approached the president for more weapons and equipment. With what Mick had brought from the Zoo, they had the firepower of a Marine infantry company. What they didn't have was a company of US Marines themselves.

With Achille, who had demanded to be with the assault element, they had five trigger-pullers—two US Marines, an Australian soldier, a British SAS soldier, and a Benin ranger. And Thor, of course.

Seven rangers comprised the blocking force, three civilians were the distraction, and five would rescue the jungle wives and any youngsters. Facing them were at least twenty-two mercs.

This wouldn't be a cakewalk.

Thor grunted beside him and he said, "Stay alert, boy."

"He is alert, Charles. He's anxious to get on with the hunt," Achille explained.

He frowned, careful to keep his face turned away from the ranger. The man seemed to know what Thor was thinking much better than he could. He had mentioned healing quickly from a gunshot wound after Thor licked him. The goop—the substance seemingly in all Zoo plants and animals—might have healing power for all he knew. Could it be possible that the goop did something with the demiwolves along those lines?

Reen, who monitored the civilians, gave them a thumbs-up. Booker nodded and signaled the group to move out. He looked into the afternoon sky. There was a good possibility that this would be the last afternoon sky he'd ever see.

He'd find out in a few short hours.

Charles sat behind the M2 Browning, ready for bear. He'd been surprised that the Benin Army even had the .50 caliber machine gun in its T/O. He'd expected the RPGs and Type 56 assault rifles the president had scrounged for them. The M2 was an old weapon but it packed a powerful punch. With the armor-piercing rounds, it could even destroy the Chinese Type 63 APC that stood at the side of the camp.

He looked through his NVDs at four mercenaries who chatted around a campfire and passed a bottle between them. At forty-five minutes before sundown, the civilians had begun to cut trees a klick away. Achille had protested at first, but they needed something to divide the mercenary force. When the first thwacks of axes reached the camp, it had taken them ten minutes before eight were dispatched to take care of the interlopers—eight mercs who were not in camp now.

The three civilians had stopped chopping a few minutes before and should have hightailed it out of there. The other five were positioned to the east side of the camp. Their task was to get the jungle wives and any children out of the camp when the shooting started.

As if on cue, one of the mercenaries walked out of the jungle leading a young girl. He chained her to a tree with the others and joined his comrades. Charles couldn't hear them but he didn't have to. The way the man thrust his hips and laughed was more than graphic enough to convey his meaning, even two hundred meters away.

He would much rather be farther out. His M2 had an effective range of one thousand eight hundred meters, after all. But with the bush, they were lucky to have as much distance as they did. The mercenaries were either very confident or very unprofessional. They'd selected their hide with ease of access in mind, not security.

At a rustle in the grass in front of him, he grabbed his Remington .12 gauge, but it was only Mick returning. As soon as darkness had given him cover, he'd placed the claymores and brought the wire back with him. Five of them gave overkill to the camp but left a safe zone around the jungle wives. Another four had been positioned along the route the eight had taken to investigate the sound of chopping wood.

Like the M2, the M18 Claymore was an oldie but

goodie. Each directional anti-personnel mine fired seven hundred steel balls about one hundred meters in a sixty-degree arc. Mick had crept in closer than fifty meters, so aside from a few shrubs and a couple of scraggly trees, the mines should devastate the camp. If all went well, there wouldn't be that much for them to clean up.

As if it ever goes well.

"Let's do this," Booker whispered.

Charles, with the big M2, remained in position. The Browning was a two-man-crew-served weapon but they didn't have enough bodies. As the largest and strongest of the group, he'd been given the machine gun. Booker, Mick, Reen, and Achille spread out to their firing positions.

Thor looked up when Achille left but he stayed beside Charles, who released a little breath of relief.

Spread out with about fifteen meters between them, they needed NVDs to see each other. They each gave Booker a thumbs-up, and he gave one to Mick. The Australian pulled the detonator.

The American closed his eyes and turned away. A moment later, the fires of hell erupted at the mercenary camp. He looked back up and his NVDs had to darken to protect his vision. Smoke and dust covered the location.

Charles already had the Browning locked in on the APC, and he delivered a fusillade of armor-piercing rounds into it. Sparks erupted off the vehicle as the .50 caliber rounds turned it into Swiss cheese.

The smoke began to clear. The four who'd been around the campfire were blots on the ground. All the tents were down, and the stack of supplies was shredded. Two men stumbled to their feet from the remnants of the tents. He swung off the APC and eliminated the second as one of his companions had already taken care of the first.

At his side, Thor jumped up and whined.

"Stay!" Charles yelled as he poured more fire into the camp and the big Browning chewed up what was left. The NVDs were not the same as seeing during daylight but still, he thought he should see more bodies.

It took a moment, but he soon realized he'd been right. Return fire issued from deeper into the camp. They'd hoped all the mercs would have been asleep or on watch but evidently, some had been down at the riverside where they'd been in defilade to the assault element's fire.

The mercs might not have NVDs, but the line of the Browning's tracers was a reverse arrow that pointed directly at him. The mercenaries concentrated their fire on him, and rounds whistled ominously over his head. Charles swung his barrage to sweep the back of the camp when at least one mercenary adjusted on him. Two rounds clanked off the Browning and made him flinch, but he maintained the onslaught.

An explosion of pain rocked him as another round caught his left hand on the grip. He pulled back and whipped his hand in pain, which spattered blood over him and Thor.

"Damn!" he shouted and looked at his hand. His little finger was pulverized and the one beside it gouged and bleeding. The entire hand was numb. He tried to reach up to fire, but the hand wouldn't cooperate.

"No problem. I've still got my right hand," he muttered and tried to fight off the nausea that threatened to overtake him.

The M2 Browning could be triggered with either thumb but aiming the big gun with one hand was more difficult.

"The civilians!" Reen shouted.

Charles fired another burst and turned to see one of their civilian rescue team fall as a mercenary bolted to the chained girls. He snatched one and tried to pull her away, forgetting that she was still attached to the others.

He began to swing his Browning around, but with the man holding the girl, he couldn't actually fire and neither could the others. Two hundred meters was nothing to a trained Marine or soldier, but at night and with a struggling girl, none wanted to risk the shot.

"Kill, Thor," Achille shouted.

Charles reached for the demiwolf but he was too slow. Thor surged away and bounded across the intervening distance.

"Don't hit Thor!" he shouted and released another burst into the camp, well away from Thor's approach.

Distant firing caught his attention. The rangers had engaged, but there wasn't much that he could do. With so few people and Booker not wanting to endanger the rangers and civilians, there hadn't been much in the way of planning for mutually supporting fire.

He continued to fire but his gaze was locked on Thor as he streaked across to the area. The mercenary didn't have NVDs, but as the animal broke into the camp, he must have seen something. He spun and fired in the same moment that Thor leaped.

The demiwolf caught the man high, thrust him back, and separated him from the struggling girl. He flailed at his attacker and Charles activated the magnification in time to see Thor lean forward, his jaws wide, to crush the man's face. His arms fell limp, and the animal howled in victory.

"Way to go, buddy!" Charles shouted before Thor staggered two steps and fell.

Another mercenary stood to fire at the wounded animal, but the American was faster and the big .50 cal rounds almost cut the body in two.

He was barely aware as two more civilians broke from cover to try to free the girls. His rage flowed through him, his mangled finger forgotten, and he poured fire into every inch of the camp. The barrel began to glow a dull red, and it wasn't until there was a blast behind him that he snapped back to reality.

The eight who had run off to check the distraction had returned. For once, a plan had worked and the claymores placed there had done their job. There were three measured shots as Reen or Booker finished any survivors.

Quiet descended on the battlefield and a low mist of propellant smoke swirled slowly across the ground.

"Charles," Booker shouted, then repeated the call when he didn't answer. "Check on the rangers."

He stared at Thor on the ground for a moment and picked the walkie talkie up with his right hand.

"Rambo, what's your status?"

"Uh...one dead, Charles," Rambo said, his voice unsteady.

"Friendly or enemy?" he snapped.

"Poitier. He's dead. Two of the poachers are now, too. They surprised us," he said. "I'm sorry."

"One dead. Poitier. Two mercs," Charles yelled to Booker.

He could switch frequencies and tell him over the walkie talkie, but this was easier.

"I'm checking on Thor."

"Wait," the Brit said.

"I'm going." He picked his Remington up with his good right hand and stood.

"Bleddy hell," Booker muttered and said, "Reen, go with him while Mick checks the ones behind us. Achille and I'll cover you."

Charles stalked across the ground, the muzzle of his 12-gauge seeking a target hungrily. He glanced continually at Thor, and that was almost his undoing.

Reen was alert, however, and she fired a three-round burst into the merc who'd played possum an instant before he shot her teammate.

The American looked at the dead boy only fifteen meters away and muttered, "Thanks."

"Keep your head on, Marine," she retorted.

His heart was in his throat as he approached Thor's inert body. He knelt over it and tears clouded his eyes as he put his hand on his back. The big head moved and licked his left hand.

Two red eyes looked at him.

A metallic clink surprised him, and he swung his Remington up and froze the civilian who'd finally cut through the chain. He lowered his shotgun, and six faces stared at him, their eyes wide. No, his mind amended dully. Stared at them.

It was only then that he noticed Thor's disguise had

fallen off. They could see his horns and they could see his eyes. They knew this wasn't some ugly dog.

Charles didn't care. He picked Thor up, who whined in pain. Blood soaked the demiwolf's shoulder, blue Zoo blood that mixed with red human blood from his hand.

"A dupe, Aja," the girl Thor had saved said as he carried him out of the camp.

CHAPTER TWENTY-EIGHT

Thor

"You tell Sophie I'm sorry for dragging you here," Charles said as Booker stood at the SUV.

"You need to tell her yourself, Yank." Booker said. "I can't convince you to come with me? The baby's due in a month, you know. I know you wanted to stay here for a couple of weeks, but there's still time after that to be there."

"I wouldn't know what to do with a baby," he said. "Besides…" he added and inclined his head toward Thor.

He never heard his name, but he knew Charles was talking about him. He wagged his tail and thumped it on the porch.

"Come here, then, big man," Booker said and pulled him in for a hug. "You do need to come and visit Edinburgh. There's some big arts festival there for the entire month. Biggest arts festival in the world."

"You like the arts?" he asked and Reen scoffed.

"I'm a family man, now, Yank. Got to up the fancy folk shit."

"If you two are quite done with your love fest, come here," she said.

She hugged him harder than Booker had and his ribs protested.

"They could come back, you know," she whispered.

"President Okunkuo said he rounded up all the ring leaders, even that Burkina Faso general. We should be safe."

"You believe that? There's always bad guys out there."

"It will be okay."

"And you're one-handed. Maybe I should stay."

"Roo will get out of his bed and come down to kill me if I let you stay."

"Hey, we're not a thing," she protested.

"Yeah, you keep saying that."

She gave him the finger and climbed into the back seat. "Keep your powder dry," she said through the open window.

Mick and Achille had talked quietly while the other two had said their goodbyes. They shook hands, and the Australian came over to give Charles a whack on the back.

"You watch out for him," he said and pointed at Achille. "I might be back sooner rather than later. I think I could learn to like it here. *O dabọ, ọrẹ,*" he said to Achille before he climbed into the driver's seat.

"Learning the local language, I see," the American said with a laugh.

"Durn tootin', Pilgrim," Mick said in an excellent John Wayne imitation as he put the SUV into gear.

Achille stepped up to stand beside Charles and a moment later, Thor pushed his way between them. The wound in his shoulder had already healed but he'd milked it for the last two days and basked in the attention.

The three watched as the SUV made its way down the drive.

"I spoke with Hounsou this morning. They are feeling powerful to drive the poachers out."

"They weren't only poachers, Achille," Charles said. "And the villagers had quite a bit of help," he added, patting Thor on the head.

"True, but this is the first time they've stood up like this."

There was a long moment of silence as the two humans stared down the empty drive.

"And?" Charles asked.

Thor looked up, knowing that he was now the subject of their conversation.

"He's an orisha. Even the witch doctor says so. One of Aja's sons, they think. Someone to protect the forest."

Somehow, he understood that the friend-humans thought he should protect this land and the animals in it. The thought was…satisfying.

He still wasn't sure how he understood Achille and was now beginning to understand Charles, even when he didn't understand most of the sounds they made. All he knew was that there was now a connection between them.

"That could be a problem," Charles said.

"Or a blessing."

"If people—certain people with power—realize he's here, they will come after him. He would be too valuable, a domesticated, uh…"

"Alien. I know. From that missile the scientists studied."

The American shrugged.

"I'd like to know more about that," Achille said and his hand strayed to Thor's back as well.

"I'll tell you everything."

There was another long silence before Achille said, "You're not really planning on going back in a couple of weeks, right?"

Thor tensed and looked at him. This was the question that had tugged at his mind for the last two days.

"So, you're reading my mind now, too? Like Thor here?"

"And?"

Charles laughed and said, "No, I'm planning on staying a while."

Thor's tail thump, thump, thumped on the ground.

"I've got more than enough money from the BOHICA Warriors, and I'm still a one-third owner. I'm thinking this is a good place to stay for a long while. Got to manage this place. Can't trust the hired help to keep from taking on all the bad guys in the world, you know."

"Well, boss," Achille said, "What now?"

A stick came out of the trees to catch Charles on the top of the head. Thor looked up to where Mr Ogbé stared at them through the leaves.

The big man picked the stick up and turned it over in his hand before he dropped it. He looked up, chuckled, and said, "Maybe we teach the residents a few manners, Achille. How about that? But for now, what say we get some lunch?"

The three turned and walked to the station.

For the first time in a long, long time, Thor was totally content. He had his pack.

AUTHOR NOTES - JONATHAN BRAZEE

When Michael and I first discussed The BOHICA Chronicles over tacos last year, Thor wasn't in the equation. It wasn't until we started working out the beats that Thor first surfaced, and over the next three books, he became a major focus on the Zoo and its relationship with humanity. Like most of you readers, I fell in love with him.

Writing Book 2 was rough, and I already knew how Book 3 would reunite Thor and Charles. I know what transpired stressed out many of you, but I hope you were happy with how things worked out.

Readers contacted me, however, wanting more of Thor, and I realized that I wasn't done with him. So, while C.J. was putting the finishing touches of Book 3, I wanted to continue the story of Thor in my own words, and only my own words. I discussed it with Michael, and started typing away.

This is the result.

Jonathan Brazee
North Las Vegas, 2019

CONNECT WITH THE AUTHORS

Jonathan Brazee Social

Website:

http://jonathanbrazee.com/

Email List:

http://eepurl.com/bnFSHH

Facebook Here:

https://www.facebook.com/jonathanbrazeeauthor/

Michael Anderle Social

Website:

http://lmbpn.com

Email List:

http://lmbpn.com/email/

Facebook Here:

www.facebook.com/TheKurtherianGambitBooks/

www.facebook.com/groups/320172985053521/ (Protected by the Damned Facebook Group)

OTHER ZOO BOOKS

BIRTH OF HEAVY METAL

He Was Not Prepared (1)

She Is His Witness (2)

Backstabbing Little Assets (3)

Blood Of My Enemies (4)

Get Out Of Our Way (5)

APOCALYPSE PAUSED

Fight for Life and Death (1)

Get Rich or Die Trying (2)

Big Assed Global Kegger (3)

Ambassadors and Scorpions (4)

Nightmares From Hell (5)

Calm Before The Storm (6)

One Crazy Pilot (7)

One Crazy Rescue (8)

One Crazy Machine (9)

One Crazy Life (10)

One Crazy Set Of Friends (11)

One Crazy Set Of Stories (12)

SOLDIERS OF FAME AND FORTUNE

Nobody's Fool (1)

Nobody Lives Forever (2)

Nobody Drinks That Much (3)

Nobody Remembers But Us (4)

Ghost Walking (5)

Ghost Talking (6)

Ghost Brawling (7)

Ghost Stalking (8)

Ghost Resurrection (9)

Ghost Adaptation (10)

Ghost Redemption (11)

Ghost Revolution (12)

THE BOHICA CHRONICLES

Reprobates (1)

Degenerates (2)

Redeemables (3)

Thor (4)

CPSIA information can be obtained
at www.ICGtesting.com
Printed in the USA
BVHW081025150320
575062BV00001B/171